Lisa B. Kamps

loving HARD

Chesapeake Blades
Book 2

Lisa B. Kamps

Lisa B. Kamps

For Jami Davenport and Kate Willoughby

Thanks for the friendship, laughter, insight, and late-night chats.

Let the meeting begin…!

Loving Hard
Copyright © 2018 by Elizabeth Belbot Kamps

All rights reserved. Except for use in any review, the reproduction or utilization of this work in whole or in part in any form by any electronic, mechanical or other means, now known or hereafter invented, including xerography, photocopying and recording, or in any information storage or retrieval system, is forbidden without the express written permission of the author.

The Chesapeake Blades™ is a fictional semi-professional ice hockey team, its name and logo created for the sole use of the author and covered under protection of trademark.

All characters in this book have no existence outside the imagination of the author and have no relation to anyone bearing the same name or names, living or dead. This book is a work of fiction and any resemblance to any individual, place, business, or event is purely coincidental.

Cover and logo design by Jay Aheer of Simply Defined Art
http://www.simplydefinedart.com/

All rights reserved.
ISBN: 1983756997
ISBN-13: 978-1983756993

contents

Title Page iii
Dedication v
Copyright vi
Other titles by this author ix
Dear Reader: xi

prologue 13
chapter one 16
chapter two 25
chapter three 33
chapter four 43
chapter five 52
chapter six 62
chapter seven 70
chapter eight 78
chapter nine 85
chapter ten 96
chapter eleven 101
chapter twelve 113
chapter thirteen 121
chapter fourteen 128
chapter fifteen 139
chapter sixteen 150

chapter seventeen	165
chapter eighteen	173
chapter nineteen	184
chapter twenty	192
chapter twenty-one	198
chapter twenty-two	207
chapter twenty-three	214
chapter twenty-four	222
chapter twenty-five	230
chapter twenty-six	241
chapter twenty-seven	246
epilogue	255
About the author	259
CROSSING THE LINE preview	261
PLAYING THE GAME preview	267

Other titles by this author

THE BALTIMORE BANNERS

Crossing The Line, Book 1
Game Over, Book 2
Blue Ribbon Summer, Book 3
Body Check, Book 4
Break Away, Book 5
Playmaker (A Baltimore Banners Intermission novella)
Delay of Game, Book 6
Shoot Out, Book 7
The Baltimore Banners 1st Period Trilogy (Books 1-3)
The Baltimore Banners 2nd Period Trilogy (Books 4-6)
On Thin Ice, Book 8
Coach's Challenge (A Baltimore Banners Intermission Novella)
One-Timer, Book 9
Face Off, Book 10
First Shot At Love (A Baltimore Banners Warm-up Story)
Game Misconduct, Book 11
Fighting To Score, Book 12
Matching Penalties, Book 13

THE YORK BOMBERS

Playing The Game, Book 1
Playing To Win, Book 2
Playing For Keeps, Book 3
Playing It Up, Book 4
Playing It Safe, Book 5
Playing For Love, Book 6
Playing His Part, Book 7

Lisa B. Kamps

THE CHESAPEAKE BLADES

Winning Hard, Book 1
Loving Hard, Book 2
Playing Hard, Book 3
Trying Hard, Book 4
Falling Hard, Book 5

FIREHOUSE FOURTEEN

Once Burned, Book 1
Playing With Fire, Book 2
Breaking Protocol, Book 3
Into The Flames, Book 4
Second Alarm, Book 5

STAND-ALONE TITLES

Emeralds and Gold: A Treasury of Irish Short Stories
(anthology)
Finding Dr. Right, Silhouette Special Edition
Time To Heal
Dangerous Passion

Dear Reader:

Welcome to the second book of The Chesapeake Blades!

If you read the first book, you'll realize that Sammie's story is a little different from Taylor's and she's dealing with some issues of her own. Yes, the issues with fighting to find a place of their own in the sports world still exists, but the larger focus for this book has shifted a little.

Sammie is a single mother juggling the obligations of a full-time job in addition to playing hockey. And, like a lot of mothers out there, she worries that her young daughter is paying the price of her busy schedule. But with help from her friends—and support from a surprising source—her struggles become a little easier to deal with.

I hope you enjoy meeting the ladies of The Blades, and that you cry and cheer with them on their journey. Shannon's story is next, and I'm so excited to get started on it—I have a feeling she might surprise all of us!

And if you're interested in learning more about the NWHL, please check out their website at www.nwhl.zone!

Happy Reading!

LBK

#FightLikeAGirl
#PlayLikeAGirl

Lisa B. Kamps

prologue

Air, dry and acrid, filled Jonathan Reigler's lungs with each breath he sucked in through his clenched teeth. He tightened his grip on the rifle and looked over the shoulder of the man sitting in front of him.

He couldn't meet his eyes. If he did, the man would see what this was costing him.

What the last few months had already cost him.

Loud bursts of gunfire, shattering the silence of the desert.

Screams and cries as bullets ripped into flesh.

Blood, dark and red, saturating the sand beneath his feet.

An outstretched hand, the palms scratched and caked with dirt. Lifeless fingers reaching across the desert floor, stretching toward the switch that would kill them all.

Dark eyes, opened to the searing sun beating above them, the sightless eyes focused on something nobody else could see.

The face, young and unlined, the skin oddly perfect, marred only by the blood seeping from the boy's mouth.

A boy. A fucking kid. No more than ten or eleven. Lifeless.

Because of Jonathan.

The boy wasn't the first one. Far from it. Jonathan

feared he wouldn't be the last. But there was something about *this* body, something about this last mission that—

He sucked in another breath, the sound no more than a hiss in the stuffy air of the closed tent. Ignore it. Ignore the image, ignore the memories.

Forget everything.

Just…forget.

The man across from him finally looked away, his gaze shifting to the papers scattered on the dusty surface of the desk in front of him. "Are you sure you want to do this?"

"I don't have a choice." He thought he had, all those months ago. Thought he'd be able to separate the two lives he'd been living. The two men he'd become. But he couldn't. Not anymore.

He blinked away the image of wide brown eyes, shining with laughter. Pushed away the ghost-memory of warm hands caressing his body. Made himself forget the soft words whispered with a warm breath against his ear.

I love you, Jon. We'll be waiting for you.

Ignored the pain that ripped through him when the memories shattered what was left of his soul.

Jonathan cleared his throat and repeated the words. "I don't have a choice."

"There's always a choice."

"No, sir. Not in this. Not anymore."

The older man sighed, the sound filled with weariness. He grabbed a pen, scrawled something on the bottom line of a ragged sheet of paper, then held the pen out to Jonathan.

"You don't have to do this, Sergeant. You're still her husband."

Jonathan grabbed the pen, his fingers tightening around it for the briefest second before he scrawled his signature on the paper that would completely sever the man he'd been from the man he'd become.

Her husband?

Maybe. Once upon a time. But not now. Not anymore.

Now, he was a monster.

chapter ONE

Two Years Later

Sweat dripped from her face and hit the ice, evaporating in an unnoticed wisp of steam. Sammie bit down on the mouth guard and leaned forward, her legs pumping as the blades of her skates tore across the ice.

Shouts—yells and screams of encouragement—disappeared in the rush of blood that echoed in her ears. Push. Harder. Faster.

She closed in on the player from Richmond. Closer. Closer still. But it wasn't close enough, the other woman was going to score—

Not if she had anything to do with it.

Sammie gave one final push and hurled her body through the air with a loud grunt, blocking the puck before it could reach the net. She heard a sharp thud and felt her flesh sting as the puck connected with her jaw just before her body crashed to the ice. Silence and then the sound of a horn splitting the air, accompanied by cheers and applause.

Holy crappola, that hurt. That really hurt. She rolled to her side and pushed up on one elbow as she looked around. Shannon Wiley, their goalie, was racing from the net, a broad smile on her flushed face. And here came Taylor LeBlanc and Dani Baldwin, two of her teammates. They were wearing the same goofy smiles on their faces as they slid to a stop next to her, spraying her with snow. Hands grabbed her, clapping her on the back and helping her from the ice all at the same time. Sammie nodded, shook her head once, then almost stumbled before she regained her balance.

Ouch. Yeah. That was definitely going to leave a mark.

But it was worth it. She stopped that last shot. The Blades won.

"Way to go, Reigler."

"Holy fucking shit, Sammie. You were airborne." Shannon leaned forward and butted her helmet against Sammie's, then patted her on the shoulder so hard, Sammie stumbled again. "Totally airborne. It was abso-fucking-lutely beautiful."

They moved back to the bench as one, all six of them: Sammie and Shannon and Taylor and Dani. Sydney Stevens and Stephanie Mason. All talking at once, drowning out Coach Reynolds's congratulations as they headed off the ice.

Sammie rubbed her jaw and looked around, her gaze coming to a rest on the guy who had been filming the game. "Do you think he caught it on camera?"

"Yeah. Sure. He must have, right?"

"And if he didn't, I'm sure someone did. I'll ask Chuckie later tonight."

Sammie nodded and pushed her way into the locker room with everyone else, the noise of their excited conversation louder in the small room. Everyone was still talking all at once, their excitement at winning another game a living, breathing thing.

Sammie accepted more congratulations then headed over to the bench and started pulling off her gear: helmet, jersey, pads, skates, shorts. She folded everything and neatly placed the equipment in her gear bag, then leaned back on the bench to stretch. Taylor dropped down beside her and leaned forward, her brows lowered over eyes the color of whiskey.

"Look up."

"What?"

"You heard me. Look up." Taylor nudged Sammie's chin with the tip of two fingers. "Yup, thought so. You need a bandage or something."

"I do?"

"Yeah. You're bleeding."

Sammie brushed at her chin then looked down at the blood smeared on her fingertips. "Is it bad?"

"Not too bad. You don't need stitches or anything. Maybe an ice pack, though, because it's already swelling and bruising."

"Yeah?" Sammie tried to stop the smile threatening to break free but failed. Her first real game-related injury. Wasn't that something to be proud of? She reached behind her and pulled the phone from her bag, then tossed it to Taylor. "Here, take a picture."

"Seriously?"

"Yes, seriously. I need to have a picture of this and I'm the worst at selfies."

Taylor rolled her eyes but snapped a couple of quick shots. "There. Happy?"

"Yes. I know it's not a big deal to you, but this is a first for me. I need to savor the moment."

"You're such a dork."

"But I'm an adorable dork." Sammie tossed the phone back in her bag then grabbed her toiletries kit and headed for the shower room.

"You're something, alright." Taylor nudged her then headed into one of the showers.

The teasing didn't stop, not even after Sammie had finished with her own shower before receiving a butterfly bandage and an ice pack before piling out of the small rink that served as their home arena. The team was heading to The Ale House, like they did after every game the Blades played at home.

After every game? Sammie laughed to herself. This was only their fifth game, in their very first season of the not-quite-semi-pro league. It still didn't feel real, despite the scrapes and bruises and her now-throbbing chin and jaw.

She had seen the notice about try-outs for the new women's hockey league eight months ago—and had nearly ignored it. A women's hockey league? She didn't stand a chance, not when her only experience had been playing in a beer league a few years ago, in a different lifetime. She didn't have anything to offer, not like the other women she was sure would be trying out. She was short and petite. A single mother. A kindergarten teacher, for crying out loud. What could she possibly offer? What made her think she could even compete?

But the idea, once planted, wouldn't leave her. So she dug out her skates and had them sharpened, then spent several entire weekends on the ice during the public skating sessions at a rink thirty minutes away from her parents' house.

Wondering if it would be enough.

Knowing it wasn't even close to being enough.

It had been thoughts of her daughter that had followed her to the rink that morning when she went to try out. Clare, who'd had her entire life turned upside down more than two years ago. It didn't matter that she wouldn't remember, not the details, anyway. Clare was only three now. A happy, well-adjusted, handful that Sammie treasured more than anything else in the world. But she wanted more for Clare—what parent didn't? She wanted her daughter to see that women could do anything they wanted, that they didn't need a man in their lives to make them complete.

Sammie wanted to be the example her daughter could look up to.

And, by some small miracle that Sammie still didn't understand, she'd been offered a spot on the team—and a contract. No, it wasn't much, barely a couple of hundred dollars per game, money that scarcely covered the cost of equipment and practices and time away from home for their road games.

But it was something. Sammie could proudly tell everyone that she was a professional hockey player—kind of. And she had new friends—family, really. Women just like her, trying to prove to the world that they could do anything they wanted, and do it better than anyone expected.

She still couldn't believe she had nearly thrown it all away. Not just her—all of them. The entire team. They had all been prepared to quit yesterday, when they'd had a showdown of sorts with the owner.

Only time would tell if anything they'd said would make a difference, but Sammie thought it might.

And holy crappola, Sammie still couldn't believe

they'd done it, confronted the owner that way. That *she'd* done it. It shouldn't be so hard to believe, not really. She was a different person than she'd been two years ago—her daughter's life wasn't the only one that had been turned upside down.

But that was a long time ago. She needed to keep her promise to herself and not look back, needed to keep focusing forward. And for the most part, she could. It helped having family.

And friends.

Even if those friends were a little on the crazy side. Like Shannon, who once again was standing on the chair. She paused, whipped the long blonde hair from her face, then looked down at Sammie with a wide grin.

"To the D-man who made a brilliant save! Just don't get any ideas about taking over my job, Short Stuff."

The women around her laughed and cheered, raising their glasses in a toast. Sammie did the same, taking a small sip of her soda just as Shannon yelled "Heads-up."

Sammie looked up, saw a flash of black heading her way, and managed to get her hand up just in time to deflect it. The puck bounced off her wrist and rolled across the table before coming to a stop against a pitcher of beer. Shannon shook her head then jumped off the chair and reached for the puck. "Okay, I take it back. I don't have to worry about you taking over my job."

"It's not like I was expecting you to throw something at me. What is it, anyway?"

"The game puck. Duh." Shannon tossed it through the air again, an easy lob that Sammie caught this time. She stared down at it as a lump of emotion formed in her throat.

"The game puck? Really? For me?"

"Oh for fuck's sake, Reigs. Don't go getting all emotional or anything, okay?"

"I'm not." Sammie's denial only caused her teammates to laugh, which made the lump in her throat grow bigger. She blinked against the sudden burning in her eyes and reached for her soda, hoping nobody would notice the way her eyes were watering. They did, of course. She held her breath, waiting for the teasing to start again, but it didn't come.

Probably because Dani kicked Shannon under the table and told her to stop before she could start.

"I wasn't going to tease her about crying. Honest." Shannon leaned across the table, a crooked grin on her face. "I was just going to tell you I think you might have a fan."

"What? What are you talking about?"

"That guy over there. He was watching you."

Nine heads turned in the direction Shannon indicated. Sammie looked but couldn't see anyone—male or female—looking their way. And she certainly didn't see anyone who looked even a little bit interesting. "Where? I don't see anyone."

"He was just there. I swear it."

Dani grabbed the glass from Shannon's hand and held it away from her. "That's it. You're cut off. No more."

"Hey, that's my first beer. Give it back."

"No. You're seeing things."

"The hell I am. I'm telling you, there was some guy checking Sammie out."

"Yeah? Then what did he look like?"

"Tall. Dark—"

"And handsome?" Sammie finished Shannon's sentence with a giggle. "I could only hope to be so lucky."

"That's not what I was going to say." Shannon retrieved her beer from Dani then drained it one long swallow. She put the glass down, gave a small belch, then looked past Sammie, a frown on her face. "I was going to say *intense*. Or maybe *brooding*. Something like that."

"But not handsome? Gee, way to get me all excited over nothing." Sammie pushed away from the table and grabbed her small purse. "I need to go pee."

"Hang on, I'll go with you."

"Shannon, I'm a big girl. I can go by myself."

"Yeah, I know. Maybe I just need to pop the seal."

Several of their teammates groaned, but instead of taking the bait like she normally would, Shannon simply ignored them. She grabbed Sammie's elbow and started leading the way across the crowded bar, glancing over her shoulder every few feet.

Sammie tugged her arm from Shannon's grip. "What is wrong with you?"

"Me? Nothing. Why?"

"Because you're acting funny. Weird. Whatever. More than normal."

"No, I'm not. I'm just—" She hesitated, looking over her shoulder again. "I don't know. Call it a feeling."

"A *feeling*? Like what, a full bladder?"

"No. I told you, there really was a guy checking you out."

"Maybe. But he's gone now—if he was ever even there."

"He was."

"Hmm. If you say so." Sammie pushed through the restroom door then bit back a sigh at the line. Of course there was a line. There always was.

"I say so. And I told you, he looked…intense."

"Yeah. So?" Sammie shoved her hands into the front pockets of her slacks and tried to cross her legs without being obvious about it.

"So I figured maybe you shouldn't go wandering off by yourself, that's all."

"I think you're overreacting. Or seeing things. There was no guy." She held up her hand, stopping Shannon before she could say anything. "And if there was, he was probably staring at you. I mean, you were the one standing on a chair and throwing stuff. Besides, men don't stare at me."

"Why would you say that?"

"Because they don't. I don't exactly stand out, you know."

"Well, you kind of do now, with that bruise on your jaw. It looks like you went three rounds in a boxing ring and lost."

"Then that must be what your mystery man was staring at." If he even existed, which Sammie seriously doubted. Shannon was either seeing things, or just being melodramatic.

"Yeah. I guess. I still think—"

Sammie waved her off and made a mad dash toward a newly-opened stall, ignoring Shannon's laughter as she slammed the door shut.

There were more important things to worry about than Shannon's mystery-man, and this happened to be one of them.

chapter TWO

Jonathan Reigler folded his tall form into the driver's seat of the sedan and slammed the door closed. His hands curled around the steering wheel, his trembling grip tightening with each breath.

What the fuck was wrong with him? He needed his fucking head examined.

For going to the game.

For following her here.

For running out before she saw him.

Fuck.

It had been close. Too damn close. All he wanted was a closer look. To see how Sammie had changed. To see if she looked as sweet as he remembered.

She *had* changed, but not in the ways he had imagined. Her hair was still thick and luscious, but shorter. Curlier. It made her look younger, sweeter.

Vulnerable.

Did those big brown eyes still twinkle with

laughter? Yes, from what he'd been able to see, as she sat there with her teammates. But there was something else there, something that hadn't been there the last time he saw her. A wariness, maybe. A subtle caution that had never existed there before.

It had taken every last reserve of his strength not to go over and pull her soft body against his. To hold her. Breathe in her scent. To claim the lush fullness of her lips with his own. To claim *her*.

To brush his knuckles over the bruise that marred her chin. He hated seeing it, hated knowing how it must have felt. His gut had twisted when he saw it and for a brief second, he had come so close to storming over and demanding who had hurt her. The rage, the protectiveness, had consumed him in its fiery grip—for all of two seconds before he forced himself to calm down. He knew exactly what had caused the bruise, he'd been there and seen it for himself.

Nobody had hurt her.

Nobody but him.

Jonathan didn't want to leave. He wanted to stay there, just watching her from his seat across the crowded room, but he couldn't. Her teammate had seen him, had noticed him enough to actually point him out—which was a real kick-in-the-ass considering he was damn good at blending in and hiding in plain sight.

Usually.

But he couldn't let Sammie see him. Not yet. She wasn't ready. Hell, he wasn't sure if *he* was ready.

Fuck.

He dragged one hand through his hair then stabbed the keys in the ignition and started the car. The engine turned over with a gentle hum, a reminder that the car was brand new, its interior filled with that unique smell that only came with new vehicles. He glanced in the rearview mirror and bit back another curse when his gaze landed on the child seat securely strapped in the middle. Another new purchase, this one taunting him with its emptiness.

Fuck. What the fuck was he doing? Did he really think any of this would help? A new car to replace the pick-up he'd had for years. A car seat for the daughter he hadn't seen in more than two years.

Two years, eight months, and fourteen days.

He hadn't seen his wife in that same amount of time.

No, he corrected himself. Not his wife—his *ex-wife*. Sammie had been his ex-wife for two years, three months, and nine days. Ever since he signed those stupid fucking papers in the middle of that stupid fucking desert.

Because he needed his fucking head examined.

Jonathan put the car in gear and headed out of the parking lot, his eagle-eyed attention on the traffic while his mind sorted through the memories.

The mistakes.

And fuck, there were a lot of them. Too many to list. Too many sins committed, too many regrets.

Too many moments wasted.

Because he'd been a fucking coward. Then—and now.

He merged into traffic heading north on York Road, driving aimlessly, barely noticing when the landscape changed from suburbia to rolling countryside. His old stomping grounds, where he'd grown up more country than city, thanks to the rural landscape of the small farms and horse country of the close-knit community that comprised the northern part of the county. He kept driving, minutes and miles into the falling night. Further north, past the high school where his name was engraved on a plaque with the other students who had enlisted after graduation.

How many years ago? How many names? How many fucking wars and conflicts? Too many.

He hit the brakes and made a sudden left, guiding the car down a narrow country road until he reached a small parking lot at the end. How many times had he been here?

Swimming. Fishing. Drinking.

Alone. With his buddies. With Sammie.

Dozens. Hundreds.

A lifetime ago.

He climbed out of the car and made his way along the dirt path, the soles of his boots digging into the loose rock and packed earth. Each step was steady and sure—and soundless. The riverbank appeared before him, a gentle sloping of the grassy earth as it met the water. The river was shallow here, nothing more than a lazy, meandering stream cutting its way over the rocky bottom. But there, just around the bend, it got deeper. A little faster. Nothing dangerous, nothing too treacherous—just enough for a fun ride on inner tubes under the blazing summer sun.

Not that it was sunny right now. Or hot. The early November air was cold, filled with a bite that would cut even deeper in a few weeks. He jammed his hands into the pockets of his jacket and ignored the cold.

But the memories...it wasn't quite so easy to ignore them.

For the hundredth time, he asked himself what the fuck he was doing. Why was here? He'd been back in

Maryland for two months now, settling into his new job. He told himself that living here, so close to Sammie, wouldn't be a problem. He hadn't seen her since that morning more than two years ago. And it wasn't like she would want to see him. She wouldn't want to have anything to do with him. He had made sure of that—two years, three months, and nine days ago.

Who the fuck was he kidding? He could be a thousand miles away and it wouldn't help.

Hell, nothing could help anymore. He'd been a fucking ass two years ago. A real cowardly prick who had been so fucking convinced he was doing the right thing. But he hadn't been thinking right. He'd thought he was doing the right thing by letting his wife and daughter go. Thought he was being so fucking *selfless*.

What a fucking crock of shit. The only thing he'd been was a fucking coward. Scared shitless. And too fucking stupid to realize it at the time, no matter how much his buddies had tried telling him otherwise.

Two years, three months, and nine days.

Why the hell hadn't Sammie moved on in that time? She should be remarried by now, settled down with an adoring husband who doted on her and a little brother or sister for Clare.

His gut twisted, filling with bile at the thought of another man touching Sammie. At the thought of his daughter calling another man *Daddy*. Fuck. He'd kill any man who tried. It wouldn't be hard. He'd killed before. Dozens of times.

Except this was different.

Sammie was no longer his wife. And Clare, his beautiful baby girl...fuck, he was nothing more than a stranger to her. She wouldn't even remember him, she had only been an infant when he left. A sweet, precious infant. An innocent baby. What had Sammie told her about him? Did she tell Clare how he had abandoned them, cut all ties with no notice and no explanation? Or did she say nothing at all? Did Clare even ask? Did she care?

He curled his hands into fists and sucked in a deep breath. It shouldn't bother him—he had no say in anything Sammie did or said. He wasn't part of their lives anymore—his choice.

His stupid, fucking choice.

But he still didn't understand why Sammie hadn't moved on. He was grateful—more grateful than words could explain. But he still didn't understand.

She had moved back here, to live with her parents. She was teaching kindergarten, just like she'd always wanted to.

And she was playing ice hockey.

Not in a beer league, like all those years a lifetime ago. But *real* hockey. A women's professional hockey team. He wouldn't have believed it if he hadn't seen it with his own eyes.

A ghost of a smile curled one corner of his mouth. His little Sammie, playing hockey. He hadn't seen that one coming, had thought he was reading a report on some other Samantha Reigler. But no, it was his Sammie.

Good for her.

It still didn't explain why the fuck she hadn't remarried and moved on.

The phone in his back pocket vibrated. Once. Twice. Jonathan thought about ignoring it, even as he dug the phone out of the pocket and held it to his ear.

"Yeah."

"You're not thinking of jumping in, are you?"

Jonathan sighed and pinched the bridge of his nose. "Look closer, asshole. It's only a foot deep here. And is there a reason you're tracking me?"

"No. Just wondering what the hell happened back at the bar."

Jonathan turned on his heel and headed back to the car. "Nothing happened."

"Yeah. No shit. You cost me twenty bucks."

"What are you talking about?"

"Daryl bet me twenty dollars that you'd wimp out. I told him he was full of it. That there was no fucking way our boy would wimp out. That our boy was on a fucking mission and never failed. That you were going to go in there and sweep the past-and-future Mrs. Reigler off her feet—"

"Or at least over your shoulder." A second voice cut into the conversation.

Jonathan uttered a low curse as he opened the car door. "Don't you two have better things to do? It's a Saturday night. Isn't there a bar or something that needs to be terrorized?"

He could imagine the two men—his friends, buddies, brothers—sitting across from one another, chiseled faces wreathed in amusement as they fist-bumped each other.

"Later, man. After you get your lame fucking ass back here and give us a full report. And the twenty bucks you cost me. You fucking coward."

"Yeah. Whatever. Don't hold your breath." Jonathan ignored the male laughter and disconnected the call. His gaze drifted out the windshield, focusing on the absolute darkness of the cold night.

Coward.

Mac had meant the word as a joke, nothing more than good-natured ribbing between men who had seen the worst the world had to offer—and done their best to make it right.

Coward.

It wasn't a word either of his buddies would think to use to describe him. It didn't fit with their image of him. Didn't fit with the experiences they had shared. Not even close.

Coward.

No, Mac hadn't meant it that way.

But he was closer to the truth than Jonathan would ever admit.

chapter THREE

Sammie held up a pair of soft fleece pants. Pale blue, with fluffy white lambs printed on them. "Clare, sweetie. These are your favorite pajamas. Don't you want to wear them?"

"No." Clare shook her head, giggled, then dashed to the other side of the small bed.

"Come on, Boo. You need to put your jammies on."

"No!" Another shake of her head, this one strong enough to send the young girl's hair flying around her face. Sammie gritted her teeth and thought about lunging over the bed. With anyone else, the move would work—but not with Clare. The little girl would simply make another mad dash, probably between Sammie's legs before running for the door.

"Get over here. Now."

"No! No no no no." The small grin that had been on her daughter's face a few seconds ago disappeared and was promptly replaced by a frown. Wide hazel eyes narrowed in displeasure and pale pink lips pursed in determination.

Two could play that game.

Sammie balled the pajamas in her hand and placed both fists on her hips. She schooled her face into a mask of authority and stared her daughter in the eye. "Young lady, do not tell me *no*. I said get over here. Now."

Clare hesitated and looked away for a brief second, her gaze darting to the door behind Sammie—no doubt trying to figure out if she could escape.

"Don't even think about it. Now get over here and let me help with your jammies."

"Don't wanna."

Sammie almost asked her why she didn't want to, then changed her mind. Did she really want to set herself up for failure by arguing with a three-year-old? No, she didn't. She needed to set the boundaries, now, or Clare would continue to push.

And when had that had even happened? Until a week ago, her daughter had been happy. Smiling. Always willing to do what was asked of her. And then—*boom*. Just like that, almost overnight, her sweet, innocent little girl had turned into a stubborn little monster.

And they said the twos were terrible. Just proved they—whoever *they* were—had no idea what they were talking about.

"If you don't get over here right now and get these jammies on, I—" Sammie paused, trying to think of a punishment that would suit the crime. "I won't read you a bedtime story."

Tears filled Clare's eyes and her lower lip started

trembling. "Don't wanna."

"Boo. Sweetie. Come on. Just put your jammies on and I'll read you a story and then you can go to sleep. Okay?"

The tears disappeared from her daughter's eyes and that stubborn look settled over her flushed face once more. "No! No no no."

"That's it. Don't you even think about it. I told you—"

"Clare. Do as your mother says. Now."

Sammie turned at the sound of the voice behind her, unsure if she should be grateful or annoyed.

Her mother stood in the doorway, slim arms crossed in front of her, her narrow face schooled into a mask of authority. Her dark eyes, so much like Sammie's, twinkled with amusement, though. Sammie knew she was trying to be helpful, and most of the time she appreciated it. Now wasn't one of those times. Whatever stage Clare was going through, she needed to learn that her mother—that *Sammie*—was the one who set the boundaries. It was hard enough to do that when Clare spent most of her days with her grandmother. It really wouldn't happen if Sammie's mom kept intervening when Sammie was here.

"Mom, please. I've got this."

Margaret Warner shifted her gaze from Clare to Sammie, understanding flashing through her eyes. She pulled in a hasty breath and nodded, then continued down the hall. Sammie heard her footsteps on the stairs, listened as the sound drifted away as her mother walked through the house toward the family room.

Should Sammie feel guilty?

Yes.

No.

No, she shouldn't. She and her parents had reached an agreement before Sammie moved back in with them, and this situation fell under that agreement. But it would be so easy to let her mom handle this. To fall back into the role of the child herself instead of the parent. To let her parents take care of not only Clare but her as well. She absolutely could not let that happen.

She turned back to face her daughter. "Clare Margaret Reigler. Get over here right now and get these jammies on."

Sammie held her breath, waiting to see if Clare would listen or if she would throw a full-blown tantrum. Long seconds ticked by before Clare finally heaved a long-suffering sigh and made her way across the room, each step slow and heavy, as if she was walking toward certain doom.

Sammie bit back her smile then pulled Clare into her arms and carried her to the bed. Several minutes later, her daughter was dressed in her pajamas and snuggled against Sammie's side as she read her a bedtime story. And not long after that, Clare's small body relaxed, the sounds of her breathing deep and even.

Sammie closed the book and placed it on the white nightstand, then gently eased away from Clare and tucked the covers around her. So peaceful, so serene.

Sammie's heart grew in her chest, threatening to explode with the love she had for her daughter. Clare was everything to her. Her reason for breathing. Her reason for living. She was...everything.

And God, she was getting so big. Growing up every single day. Sammie reached out and smoothed the curls from Clare's face then brushed her knuckles against the soft skin of her sleep-flushed face. It wasn't quite as round as it had been, even a few short months ago. Her little girl was growing up, becoming her own little person.

Sammie blinked against the tears burning her eyes then eased away from the bed, her steps soft so she wouldn't disturb Clare. She palmed the light switch, throwing the room into shadowy darkness broken only by the small nightlight in the corner, then pulled the door closed behind her.

Her parents looked up when she entered the family room a few minutes later. Her mother sat in the corner of the overstuffed sofa, legs curled under her, her finger holding the spot in the book she was reading. Her mother was so much like Sammie in build and looks, with dark curly hair threaded through with fine strands of silver hair, barely noticeable among the highlights she'd added a few weeks ago.

Her father was in his usual spot in the recliner, the open paper spread across his lap ignored in favor of the television. Sammie glanced at the flat screen television mounted on the wall, not surprised to see that some war documentary was flashing across the screen. He reached for the remote and nudged the volume down.

"Did you get her all settled in?"

"Yes, finally." Sammie flopped onto the loveseat with a sigh and a small smile. "She's really starting to become a handful, testing those boundaries."

"Just like you did when you were her age."

Sammie glanced at her mom and frowned. "Me? You said I was a happy, quiet baby."

"Baby, yes. Toddler..." Her mom's voice trailed off as she shared a conspiratorial look with her father.

"Maybe not so much."

"Don't worry. Clare will outgrow it just like you did. It's just a stage."

"I know. I just didn't expect her to flip the switch so quick, you know?" Sammie leaned to the side and grabbed her e-reader from the end table, but instead of turning it on, she just sat there, staring at nothing.

"Everything okay, Sam?"

"Hm?" She looked up and noticed her father watching her, his brow creased in a small frown. Which meant absolutely nothing, because her father always looked like that, like he was trying to figure out the solution to some puzzle only he could see. Her mom always laughed and teased him about it, then told everyone it came from living in a house full of women.

Her father shifted his bulk in the chair as he carefully folded the newspaper, making sure each crease was crisp and perfect. "You just looked like you were in deep thought."

"No, just zoning, I guess. Reviewing my schedule for this week. Wondering what I was forgetting to do. Things like that."

"Anything on the schedule other than the usual?"

"No. Work. Practice Tuesday and Thursday. Game on Saturday." Should she tell them about the interview she was supposed to be doing with one of the local papers Tuesday night? No, they'd only ask a million different questions and make a big deal out of it. At least, a *bigger* deal.

Sammie was going to be interviewed about playing on the team, about how important it was to be playing for the Blades and how she juggled the team, working full-time, and being a single parent. She was nervous enough about it, worried that she'd say all the wrong things. Having her mom and dad ask about it would only make it worse.

"At home? Maybe we can bring Clare since we had to miss it yesterday."

Sammie frowned, trying to figure out what she missed. Oh, that's right. They were talking about the game this weekend. "Yes, home. We're playing Philly."

"Maybe we should go, take Clare—"

"Thanks, Dad, but don't worry about it. She's got her heart set on going to that matinee you promised to take her to." Just one more thing Sammie seemed to be missing out on lately. "That would make for a really long day. For all of you, but especially for Clare."

"And what about you? All your days are pretty long, it seems. How are you holding up?"

"Fine. Everything's fine." So what if she was tired? This was still new to her, juggling work and hockey and weekend schedules. She'd get used to it.

"Are you sure you don't want us to bring Clare next weekend? I just hate that we had to miss the game yesterday."

"It's not a big deal. Honest."

"It is to us. We're proud of you. We want you to know that."

"I do know." Sammie swallowed against the lump growing in her throat and offered her dad a small smile. What was with her today? She wasn't usually this emotional, not really. Maybe she was just overly tired. Maybe she should go upstairs and go to sleep instead of sitting down here to read.

"How's your jaw feeling?"

"Better." And it was—for the most part. As long as she was careful and didn't chew on her right side, or accidentally hit it somehow, she barely noticed it. At least, until she looked in the mirror. Then she couldn't help but notice it, not when it was a slightly-swollen purple blotch that stood out against her fair complexion.

That didn't mean she had any intention of hiding it with makeup or anything. She was proud of the bruise, proud of how she'd gotten it. It made her feel like a professional athlete, wearing a badge of honor.

"If you need more ice, let me know. I made sure there were extra cold packs in the freezer."

"I'm fine. Really." Sammie placed her e-reader back in its normal spot then pushed to her feet. "I think I'm going to head up. Maybe get an extra hour of sleep."

"Already?" Her mother glanced at her watch then looked back at Sammie. "It's not even seven-thirty yet. Are you sure everything's okay?"

"I'm positive, Mom. It's just been a long weekend." She leaned over and pressed a kiss to her mother's cheek, then did the same to her dad as she passed. She didn't miss the concerned looks they exchanged, or her mother's quiet murmur of worried words as she left the room.

Sammie wanted to reassure them again that nothing was wrong. That she was simply tired. And that was the truth. A little more tired than usual, maybe, but nothing to worry about. It was just the frantic schedule. Teaching every day then hurrying to practice twice a week for several hours to prepare for the weekend game—all while making sure she carved out enough precious time for Clare.

At least being busy made sure she didn't have time to think about how lonely she was. About how lonely she'd been for the last two years.

Yeah, she definitely needed some extra sleep. A good night's sleep would help with all these ridiculous, morose thoughts she'd been having lately.

Sammie had just placed her foot on the bottom step to head upstairs when she heard the knock on the front door. Hesitant at first, like whoever was there was afraid of disturbing the household. Then louder, a little more determined somehow.

Knock. Knock knock. Knock.

Sammie glanced at her watch and frowned, wondering who might be stopping in for a visit at this hour on a Sunday night. They didn't have any close neighbors, not up here in the mostly rural area of the north county.

Sammie backtracked to the front door, curiosity eating at her. Maybe a stranded motorist had somehow found their long drive. Or maybe it really was one of the neighbors, stopping by to borrow something or see her dad for some reason. He was retired from his veterinary practice now, but he still offered help if any of their neighbors needed it for any of their animals.

She turned the knob then tugged on the door, a small smile of greeting on her face. The smile faltered then quickly died as the blood froze in her veins. Her lungs seized, forcing the air from her chest, making it impossible for her to breathe. The sounds of a million crickets filled her ears, obscuring all other sounds. No, not crickets. Bees. Wasps. Loud and buzzing, dangerous, the sound growing louder with each passing second as she stood there, her fingers curled in a death grip around the edge of the door.

It couldn't be. She was hallucinating. Seeing things. She was caught in a nightmare. All she had to do was force herself to wake up, and this would all be over.

But she wasn't in a nightmare. At least, not a sleeping one. And instead of waking up, Sammie was very much afraid she was close to passing out. She tightened her grip on the door, using it to prop herself up as she stared at the man in front of her through the haze of gray filling her vision.

Jon.

chapter **FOUR**

Jon.

Her mouth moved, but no sound came out. Jonathan didn't need to hear his name, not when he could read it on her lips.

Jon.

A single syllable. Three little letters. Silent yet so powerful.

It was like a fucking punch in his gut, robbing him of air and nearly doubling him over. Coming here had been a mistake. An impulse that he'd been powerless to ignore. And now that he was here, standing in front of his ex-wife, all he wanted to do was turn around and run away.

Just like he'd done two years ago.

But he couldn't, not when Sammie stood before him, her knuckles a stark white against the edge of the door she was holding so tightly. The color drained from her face and for one horrifying second, he was afraid she was going to faint. Her free hand shot toward the doorframe as her eyes closed and her knees buckled.

Jonathan didn't think, just reacted. He reached for her, his hands closing around her waist. Supporting her, keeping her on her feet.

It was the worse fucking thing he could have done.

Heat seared him, from the palms of his hands where they rested on her waist all the way through to the soles of his feet. Flames of yearning licked every inch of his body, touching parts of him he'd thought dead and buried these last two long years. Since before then, even.

Two years, three months and ten days.

But that's not why he shouldn't have touched her. It wasn't *his* reaction that startled him, it was hers.

She stiffened and tried to step back, batting his hands away. Her face filled with the heat of the same anger that flashed in her narrowed eyes. Her mouth no longer silently formed his name but rather pinched in distaste, a scowl of such ferocious revulsion that Jonathan took a quick step back and nearly knocked the screen door off its hinges.

And fuck, she was going to slam the door in his face. He could see it as surely as he could see that brief spark of hatred in her eyes. But he couldn't let her do that, no matter how much he deserved it, so he stepped forward and wedged the toe of his boot against the bottom of the door.

"Sammie." He said her name, silently winced at the hoarse desire and need in that single word. It made him sound weak. Pathetic. Begging.

And he was. All three. He'd always been that way with Sammie. Needing. Yearning. She was his biggest weakness, had always been his biggest weakness—even after he'd turned coward and fucked up everything that mattered to him.

"Sammie—"

"No. Get out. Now." She tried to close the door on him, actually stepped behind it and pushed, but it barely moved. Frustration flashed in her dark eyes, quickly followed by something that looked like desperation.

And pain.

He almost stepped back, almost let her slam the door in his face. Lord knew, he deserved a hell of a lot worse—because *he* was the one responsible for the pain she was feeling.

Coming here had been a bad idea. Stupid. Reckless. Careless. But now that he was here, he couldn't leave.

"Sammie—" He had no idea what he was going to say. *I'm sorry. Forgive me. Can we talk?* It didn't matter. He never got the chance to finish because Sammie's father came out of the family room, his gaze focused on the folded paper in his hands.

"Sam. Who's that at the—" Dennis Warner came to a halt, his eyes cold and menacing as his dark gaze met Jonathan's. The older man's body stilled and tensed, filling with anger, transforming into the rigid lines of a predator in the blink of an eye. Tense seconds passed, heavy and oppressive, filled with the underlying threat of danger.

The older man moved forward, stepping in front of Sammie, using his large body as a protective barrier.

"You're not welcome here, Jonathan."

"Mr. Warner—"

"You heard me. You need to leave. Now." The

older man's voice was pitched low, vibrating with anger and warning. Jonathan recognized it for what it was: a very real and credible threat.

"Sir. I just need to—"

"No. Get out. Now." Mr. Warner's voice grew a little louder, the anger becoming even clearer. Footsteps echoed behind the bigger man. A few seconds later, another face came into view, this one an older version of Sammie.

"Dennis? What's going on?" Mrs. Warner placed her hand on her husband's arm then peered around him. Her dark eyes widened in surprise, then quickly narrowed in confusion and dismay. "Jonathan."

She infused his name with anger and scorn, making it quite clear exactly what she thought of discovering him on her doorstep. Jonathan shifted his weight from one foot to the other, searching his mind for something to say.

But there was nothing there. Nothing he *could* say. He had no idea how much Sammie had told them about what had happened. It didn't matter, not when they obviously knew they were no longer together. Not when they knew *something* had happened—and that it was *his* fault.

"Now, Reigler. Get out. You're not—"

"Dennis, lower your voice—"

"Mom. Dad. Stop. Please." Sammie pushed between her parents, a look of mild panic on her face. "You're going to wake—"

Her mouth snapped closed and she tossed a cautious glance at Jonathan without finishing her sentence.

She didn't need to. Jonathan knew exactly what she'd been about to say: wake Clare. Their daughter.

His daughter.

And oh God, he nearly doubled over right then and there. Pain. Heartbreak. Regret. All of it and more, feelings and emotions he had no words for threatened to knock the air from his lungs and the strength from his legs. Could Sammie tell? Could she see it?

Or was he as good at hiding his emotion and pain as he thought he was, as he'd trained himself to be?

Sammie turned away from him but not before he noticed the way the muscle jumped in her bruised jaw. Her tone was calm and poised, the words barely more than a whisper as she spoke to her parents.

"Please. Let me handle this." Sammie didn't wait for their response. She reached for the coat rack just inside the door and grabbed a thick jacket, then stepped around her parents and moved outside. She pushed him out of the way as she pulled the door closed behind her then shoved her arms into the jacket. Each movement was short and brisk, filled with anger and pain that Jonathan could actually feel.

He stepped toward her. Stopped. Ran both hands down his face then jammed them into the pockets of his jeans. If he didn't, he'd be tempted to do something stupid. Like grab her. Pull her into his arms. Hold her.

Sammie didn't seem to notice the inner struggle raging inside him. Or, if she did, she didn't care. Could he blame her? No, he couldn't, not after what he'd done. Then to show up like this, unannounced and unexpected, after two years of silence? It was nothing short of miraculous that she hadn't let her father go after him.

Sammie moved to the end of the porch, out of the light and into the shadows. She leaned against the wooden railing and folded her arms in front of her then just stared at him for a long minute.

Jonathan stared back, his mind searching for something to say and immediately discarding every word. He took a hesitant step toward her then stopped when he saw the way she stiffened.

Her chin came up, defiant and proud. And her voice was firm, strong, when she spoke. "Why are you here, Jon?"

Good question. Excellent question. Why the fuck was he here? He knew why, but he couldn't tell her. Not yet.

At least not all of it. She wasn't ready. She might never be ready.

And God help him if that was the case.

"I—" He snapped his mouth closed, swallowed and took a deep breath. "I wanted to see you. See how you were doing."

And to see Clare. But he couldn't get those words past his numb lips, couldn't make himself say his daughter's name. He was so afraid of tainting her innocence with the mere act of saying her name out loud. It was irrational, he knew that. But it didn't stop how he felt, didn't keep the fear at bay.

No. He wasn't ready to see Clare, not yet. Wasn't ready to hold her, to study each little finger and toe, to see how much she'd grown. Did she look even more like Sammie now, with beautiful wide brown eyes and thick dark curls? Or did she look anything like him, with a stubborn set to her chin and a crooked smile?

Pain seared him, a pain he should be accustomed to by now. How fucking sad was it that he was so afraid to see his daughter? To see how much she'd grown and how much he'd missed the last two years? But he couldn't—not after the things he'd done. The idea of spoiling Clare's innocence with the blood on his hands left him sickened and disgusted.

He couldn't. No matter how much he wanted to. Not yet.

Maybe not ever.

Did Sammie hear his silent omission? Did she wonder about it? Or was she so consumed with her own anger that she didn't notice? Or maybe she didn't care, not with the way she stood there, her eyes burning in the shadows as she stared at him.

"To see how I was doing?" Sammie repeated his words, her voice low and ice cold.

"Yes. I—"

She clenched her jaw and straightened, anger clear in the rigid set of her shoulders. In the way that muscle jumped along her bruised cheek. "How I'm doing is none of your business. It hasn't been for the last two years, since you decided to just walk away."

"I didn't walk—"

"That's right, you didn't." Sammie's burst of laughter was cold and brittle, filled with anger and dismay. "You were already gone."

She took a deep breath, let it out with a hiss sharp enough to slice through his chest. Her gaze, bright with anger, met his then darted away—but not before he saw the glimmer of tears in their dark depths. "You didn't even have the decency to tell me to my face. To tell me what I did wrong."

He moved toward her, his arm outstretched. She flinched and stepped to the side, as if just the idea of his touch sickened her. Jonathan let his arm drop to his side, his fingers curled into a fist so she couldn't see the way they trembled. "It wasn't you, Sammie. It was never you."

"You're right. It wasn't. It took me eighteen months to figure that out." Her voice cracked and she pulled in another deep breath. He saw the way her fingers tightened against her arms, the way her short nails dug into the sleeves of the jacket. A tremor went through her. From the cold night air? Or something else?

"Sammie, I thought I was doing the right thing. I—"

"The right thing? The *right* thing?" Anger flushed her face, visible even in the shadows of the porch. She took one step toward him, then another. She uncrossed her arms and pointed at him with one trembling finger. "By divorcing me with no warning or explanation? By *abandoning* me while you were overseas? By abandoning *us*?"

"It's not—you don't understand."

"You're right. I don't. I never did. And you know what, Jon? I don't care. Not anymore."

"Sammie—"

"No!" She pushed against him with the flat of her hands. Once, twice. Once more with a grunt of frustration. Jonathan didn't move, not even when her hand curled into a fist. Let her hit him. Let her take out every ounce of hurt and pain and betrayal on him. It was the least he deserved.

But instead of hitting him, she dropped her hands to her sides and stepped around him. "Go away, Jon. I don't want to see you again. Ever. You're no longer part of our—part of *my* life. You never were."

"Sammie, please—"

His words echoed in the heavy stillness, heard only by the cold night surrounding him. Sammie was already inside, the door closed against him and anything else he might say.

Jonathan stood there for a long time, Sammie's words echoing in his mind.

You're no longer part of my life. You never were.

It wasn't the words that made his lungs seize and his gut twist—it was the sight of the tears in Sammie's eyes.

And the briefest glimpse of the truth he heard beneath the lie.

chapter FIVE

Sammie spun in a semi-circle, her feet gliding effortlessly across the ice as she skated backward. She crouched low, the blade of her stick snug against the ice as she waved it back and forth. Taylor feinted to the left then lunged to the right but Sammie had been expecting that move. She stuck with Taylor, reached out with her stick, and jabbed at the puck. She held her breath, waiting to see the puck dash free. But it didn't.

Sammie swallowed a curse and lunged for the puck once more. The blade of her left skate got caught in a gouge in the ice, throwing her off balance and kicking her leg out from under her. She stumbled, tried to catch herself, then hit the ice on her backside and kept sliding.

She came to a stop near the net, seconds before Taylor shot the puck. It tipped off Shannon's glove then plopped to the ice behind her. Sammie dropped her head with a groan then just lay there, her chest heaving with each breath.

"You okay?" Taylor came to a stop next to her then reached down and offered her a hand. Sammie ignored it as she rolled onto her stomach and pushed to her feet.

"Yeah. Stupid move. Totally stupid. I should have had that." Sammie removed her helmet then ran one gloved hand over her head.

"You and me both." Shannon skated out of the net then tapped Taylor against the leg with her stick. "That was a weak-ass shot, LeBlanc."

"Yeah. I pulled back too quick. Which means you should have really had it."

"What can I say? I was too busy watching Reigler here to make sure she didn't plow into me."

"I wasn't even close to plowing into you."

"Sure you were. That's as good an excuse as any, right?"

Sammie ignored both her teammates and turned to study the gouge that had tripped her up. "I thought they said they were going to fix the ice."

"They did. Two weeks ago, anyway. I don't think they realize how tore up it gets with everyone that uses it." Taylor nudged her helmet up then wiped a hand across her sweaty face. "It would be nice to have our own ice, wouldn't it?"

"Don't hold your breath. I don't think that's ever going to happen."

"Well, it should. I mean, you don't see the Banners sharing their ice with anyone, do you?"

"No. But we're not exactly drawing in the same kind of crowds, are we?" Disappointment laced Sammie's words, the same disappointment she knew every single one of her teammates felt. Game attendance was still below expectations, and there was still the fear that the entire league would go under. Yes, it was only their first year. Yes, the season had just started a little more than a month ago. Yes, they still had time to build up that excitement.

Maybe.

It sounded good in theory, but the reality was a bit different. They were fighting an uphill battle, trying to overcome obstacles that no men's team had ever had.

Sammie wanted to believe they were succeeding but deep down, she couldn't help but have her doubts. Her normal optimism was being challenged every day. Every week. Every game.

Or maybe her change of mood had more to do with Sunday night. She was still reeling from it, still trying to convince herself she had only imagined it.

"Hey. Earth to Sammie. Wake up."

Sammie shook her head then blinked, surprised to see Shannon waving her hand in front of her face. She blinked again then realized Taylor and Shannon were both staring at her, like they'd been trying to get her attention for several minutes.

"Are you okay? You seem out of it or something."

"Yeah. Fine."

"Are you sure? Because—"

"My ex-husband stopped by the house Sunday night." And holy crappola, she hadn't meant to tell them that. She hadn't meant to tell *anyone* that.

And from the expressions on their faces, they hadn't been expecting to hear it. They exchanged quiet glances with each other then slid in closer, blocking any chance Sammie might have had to escape.

"Deets, Reigler."

"Yeah, seriously. What happened?"

"Nothing. I don't want to talk about it."

"Oh no. No way." Shannon moved even closer and wrapped one hand around Sammie's arm to keep her in place. "You can't just drop that fucking bombshell and think you can leave. Not happening."

Sammie opened her mouth to say she could do just that then snapped it shut again. She hadn't meant to say anything, hadn't realized those words were even thinking about coming out—not that words could actually think but still...

Maybe it was her subconscious working. Maybe she *wanted* to talk about it. Or *needed* to talk about it. If that were the case, it would have to be with the two women in front of her, staring at her like she had just lost her mind.

She blew out a heavy sigh then glanced around. Practice was almost over, and then she had to do that crazy interview she had agreed to. If she were going to talk about it—about Jon—then now would be the only time.

Unless she could find some excuse to stall them until next practice. Or maybe before Saturday's game. Or maybe *after* Saturday's game or even—

No, none of that would work, not with the way Shannon and Taylor were watching her—like they were expecting her to make up some kind of excuse. Like they were ready to tackle her if she tried to make a mad dash for freedom. That's something both of the women would definitely do.

Sammie took another deep breath, held it, then slowly released it. She kept her gaze averted, staring at the toes of her skates. "There's really nothing to say. He just showed up. And then he left."

"So what happened in between that you're not

telling us?"

"Nothing. Honest." Sammie looked at both women then held up three fingers of her left hand. "I swear it."

Taylor frowned, shared a quiet look with Shannon, then shook her head. "So he, what? Knocked on your door then turned around and left? Without saying squat?"

"Well, no."

"Then what? What did he say? What did he do? Did you beat his no-good ass then throw him out?"

"No." Sammie remembered the feel of his chest beneath her hands. Hard. Broad. Solid. Warm. And oh Lord, why were her palms tingling with the memory? Why was she even remembering? She had forgotten how big Jon was, how her petite frame had always seemed so much smaller than it really was next to him.

How protected she always felt in his arms.

Stop it. Now. Just stop.

The last thing she needed to do was remember how it used to be. She needed to focus on what he'd done. How much he'd hurt her.

How he'd just left her—left both of them—with no warning. No explanation.

Sammie gave herself a mental shake. "No, I didn't beat him up or throw him out. My dad almost did, though."

"What do you mean, *almost*?"

"I—I wouldn't let him. I went outside to talk to him instead."

"Okay. And then what? What did he say?"

"Nothing really."

Taylor threw her hands up and made a soft growl of frustration. "OhmyGod, getting a story out of you is like pulling teeth. What happened? What did he say?"

"That's just it. He didn't say much of anything."

"Then why was he there? What did he want? What's he even doing back in Maryland? I thought you said he was living out of state. On the west coast or something."

"I don't know. I—I just told him I didn't want to see him again and that was it."

"So you don't even know why he was there?"

"No."

"And you didn't even ask him to explain himself? Didn't demand he tell you why he did what he did?"

"No. I just told him to leave us alone."

Shannon and Taylor exchanged another look, this one even longer. Taylor shook her head then turned back to Sammie. "What about Clare? Did he even get to see her?"

Sammie blinked against the sudden burning in her eyes and shook her head. "He, uh, he didn't even ask about her." And God, admitting that hurt. Remembering it hurt. His own daughter! And he hadn't even asked about her. Had acted like he'd forgotten all about her. But that couldn't be true. It just couldn't.

Or maybe it could. Maybe the Jon she remembered no longer existed. Or maybe—even after the last two years, after everything he'd done—she was still foolish enough to make excuses for him and harbor a tiny bit of hope, foolish enough to think there must have been some reason for him to do what he did.

Sammie couldn't afford to do that, not anymore. And she couldn't allow herself to hope—her hope had died the day she received the divorce papers.

"He seriously didn't ask about her? At all?"

"Not a word, no."

Shannon frowned, her gaze moving between Sammie and Taylor. "He, uh, he does know about her, right? I mean, I don't know all the details so—"

"Yes, he knows about her." Sammie glanced down at her hand, saw the way her knuckles turned white from the grip she had on her stick. She loosened her fingers and forced a smile to her face. "She was three months old when he deployed. I remember how—"

Sammie's voice cracked and she shook her head, trying to shake the memory of the way his eyes had teared up as he held Clare in his arms. How small she had looked, how precious, with her adorable baby-grin as she looked up at her father.

Not knowing he was leaving.

Not knowing he was never coming back. Not for her.

Not for either one of them.

"Did you, uh, say anything about that? Ask him why?"

"What?" Sammie looked up, shook her head. "No. Of course not. Like I said, I just told him to leave us—me—alone."

Taylor watched her for a long minute, her whiskey-colored eyes seeing too much. "And you think that's really going to work?"

"Yeah." Sammie cleared her throat and tried to make her voice stronger. "Yes. I do."

"You don't sound too sure of that."

"Of course, I'm sure. I told him, didn't I?"

"And you think he's going to listen to you? I mean, come on, Reigs. The man shows up at your place out of fucking nowhere. He was obviously there for a reason but you didn't let him tell you why. You think he's just going to go back into whatever cesspool of hell he crawled out of because you said so?"

"I think Shannon's right. I don't think he's just going to listen."

"Well, I think you're both wrong. I haven't seen or heard from him in over two years. I don't think that's going to change."

"Except it already has, hasn't it?"

"One time. And I told him I didn't want to see him again."

Shannon studied her, those light brown eyes too serious and completely unreadable. Then she made a small sound, not quite a laugh, and shook her head. "I think you're lying to yourself."

"I'm not—"

"I think you are. About both things."

"Both things? What are you talking about?"

"About him listening to you." Shannon lifted her stick and tapped Sammie on the back of her leg with it. "And about not wanting to see him again."

"That is so far from the truth—"

"Is it?"

"Yes. It is. It really, really is. After what he did to me? To Clare? No. Seeing him again is the last thing I want." Sammie watched both women, silently daring them to contradict her. She was telling the truth. She *didn't* want to see Jon again. Ever. Not even to ask him what happened. She didn't care. Not anymore.

Even if she hadn't been able to stop thinking about his visit. Or about how he had looked—the same, but different. More intense. Harder. Not just his body, but *him*. Like something inside him had changed.

No. No, no, no. She had to stop thinking about him like that. She had to stop thinking about him, period. She didn't care. She really, really didn't. He'd just caught her off guard, that was all.

No, she absolutely didn't want to see him again—not even to ask him what had happened. To ask him *why*. Why had he done what he did? Why had he left them that way?

"Reigler!"

Sammie snapped out of her stupor and looked across the ice to Coach Reynolds. The woman hooked a thumb over her shoulder, pointing in the direction of the glass.

"Time for your interview. Get a move on."

Sammie pulled in a deep breath and let it out in a rush, forcing all thoughts and memories of her ex-husband from her mind—or, at least, trying to. "Oh, great. I don't think I can do this."

"Sure you can. You'll be great at it."

"No, I really don't think I can. I'm going to sound stupid."

"No, you're not." Taylor spun her around and started pushing her across the ice. "Trust me, it'll be easy. And it's not like it could be anywhere near as bad as my whole interview."

"Oh, crappola. Did you really have to remind me of that?"

A local news station had sent a reporter and camera crew out before the start of the season to run a feature on Taylor and her step-dad and her uncle—both men had ties to the Baltimore Banners. Chuck Dawson, the PR Director for the Blades, had thought it would be a good way to build excitement. The entire thing had pretty much backfired, with the reporter giving her negative opinions on the team and their chances of succeeding.

"Honestly, you really didn't have to remind me."

"Oh stop. You'll be fine." Taylor kept guiding Sammie toward the door as Shannon moved around them to swing it open. The goalie whacked Sammie on the backside, a little harder than she usually did.

"Go get 'em, Reigs. And try not to think about how much you have to pee while they're interviewing you."

Sammie stumbled to a stop and turned toward Shannon with an expression of horror on her face. "Why? Why would you even say that?"

"Yeah, Shannon. That's cruel. Just cruel." But Taylor was laughing, the words coming out in breathy little gasps with each chuckle. "Now that's all she's going to be thinking about."

Sammie scowled at both of them then stepped off the ice and headed toward the two young women standing next to Chuck. She knew exactly what Shannon had been doing: trying to get her mind off her ex-husband. But it didn't work, not really.

Because she was still thinking about him. About his unexpected visit.

About a pair of dark eyes she couldn't seem to stop remembering.

Dark. Intense.

And haunted. So haunted.

chapter SIX

"This is actually a pretty good article."

"Don't care."

"Seriously, you should read it. Didn't you read it?"

Jonathan tightened his fingers around the pen, took a deep breath, then relaxed his grip. "Said I don't care."

"I think you're fucking lying."

Jonathan raised his eyes from the file on his desk, glared at Mac, then went back to pretending he was making notes. He wasn't. Hell, he didn't even know what fucking file he was looking at. For all he knew, the tip of the pen was tearing into the latest resume they had received.

His mind wasn't on work—hadn't been since he walked into the small building that housed their new offices three hours ago. He knew exactly what article Mac was talking about, had damn near committed the entire thing to memory. That didn't mean he wanted to admit it. And he sure as hell didn't feel like talking about it.

Mac obviously had other ideas because he kept rustling the damn paper and making humming noises as he read. First a mutter. Then a chuckle. Then another mutter. Jonathan blew out a deep sigh and pinned Mac with a scowl.

"I'm trying to fucking work here."

"No, you're not. You haven't been working since you walked in. Doodling isn't work."

"I'm not doodling."

"Dude. You're scribbling lines on a scrap sheet of paper that used to be my notes from the other day. You're not working."

Jonathan frowned then glanced at the wrinkled sheet of paper. He looked closer, noticing the sloppy scrawl of Mac's handwriting for the first time. Over that were deep lines and gouges, made by Jonathan's own pen. He swore under his breath, wadded the paper in his fist, then hurled it across the room.

"Fuck."

"Uh-huh. I'm thinking that's your problem. Too much build-up. You need to get that taken care of."

"Fuck you."

"Sorry, but you're not my type." Mac raised the newspaper in front of his face, but not fast enough to hide the grin. The scar that sliced across the lower part of his face turned the grin into something that looked more like a clown face—or the sinister scowl of a boogeyman.

"Don't you have something better to do?"

Mac glanced at him over the top of the paper, one dark brow raised in amusement. "Don't you?"

"Just put the fucking paper down and—"

"When I'm finished reading."

"Christ." Jonathan pushed away from the desk and grabbed a file from the stack on the cabinet behind him. It was nothing more than busy work, something to keep him from ripping the paper out of Mac's hands and shredding it to pieces.

Something to keep his mind from that stupid fucking article.

Not that there was anything wrong with the article itself. It wasn't even a full page, unless you counted the pictures. It talked about the new hockey team, the obstacles they were facing, how the Blades were competing in a market that already had a professional hockey team—the Baltimore Banners.

It could have been a total downer and filled with negativity, but it wasn't. The article focused instead on the strength and perseverance of the women on the team and talked about the spirit and gumption they needed for success.

And yeah, the writer of the article—one TR Meyers—had actually used those words: spirit and gumption. Seriously? Whatever. More power to him. Or her. That wasn't the issue Jonathan had with the article. No, his issue was on the player the article featured: Sammie.

And how they played up the fact that she was a single parent struggling to juggle her dreams of playing hockey with a full-time job, all while meeting the demands of motherhood.

Just another shot straight to his heart. One more reason for the guilt to eat at him even more than it usually did.

Fuck.

"You know, your wife is actually pretty damn cute,

especially in all that gear. She's—"

Jonathan hurled the closest object—which happened to be the pen in his hand—toward Mac. "Shut the fuck up."

The other man batted the pen away with a laugh. "Touchy, touchy."

"She's not my wife, okay? Just—fuck. Just drop it, okay? Let it go."

The door opened behind him. Jonathan spun around in the chair as Daryl walked through, a cardboard tray with three large cups of coffee balanced in one hand. He kicked the door closed behind him, his pale gaze darting between Jonathan and Mac.

"Is that the article about your wife?"

"She's not my wife."

"Not anymore. And not yet. Again. Whatever." Daryl placed the cardboard tray on the edge of Jonathan's desk then passed the coffee around. "But I think I came up with a game plan to help."

Jonathan's gut twisted and he damn near dropped the coffee. He sat the cup on his desk then leaned back and aimed a scowl at Daryl. "What the hell are you talking about? I don't need a game plan. There's nothing to *plan* for. I told you—"

"Yeah, whatever. I don't know who the fuck you're trying to kid with that bullshit lie you fed us earlier, but we know better."

Fuck.

Fuck him.

Fuck his buddies.

Fuck everything.

He should have never opened up to them. Should have never told them about Sammie. Not that they didn't already know—they did. About everything.

Because they'd been there with him, playing in that fucking sandbox. They knew exactly what he'd done because they'd given him hell about it and called him every kind of fool.

They weren't wrong. At least, not then. But now? Fuck.

Yes, he wanted Sammie back. He'd give anything to have her back. But it wasn't that fucking easy, not after what he'd done. Mac and Daryl didn't see it that way. To them, it was a simple matter of talking to Sammie and making things right.

But how the fuck could he do that without explaining why he'd done what he did in the first place? He couldn't. Hell, he couldn't even manage to string together coherent sentences in her presence—last weekend was proof of that. Showing up at her parents' place like that, unannounced and out of the blue. And then just standing there, not knowing how to say what he'd gone there to say, not even knowing what the hell he wanted to say to begin with.

Fuck.

Yeah, Mr. Warner should have thrown him off the porch face-first. It was no less than what Jonathan deserved. He was still surprised that Sammie had stopped her dad from doing just that.

Seeing her, talking to her, had been harder than he'd thought it would be. And to hear her say he was no longer part of her life…fuck, that had hurt.

Because it was true. He wasn't. He hadn't been for nearly three years. He'd been so fucking stupid back then, thinking he was doing what was best for Sammie and Clare.

And he was still paying the price, still dealing with the gaping hole in his soul.

"Do you want to fucking do this or not?"

Jonathan gave himself a mental shake and looked over. Mac and Daryl were both watching him, their shrewd gazes seeing way too much. "Do what?"

Mac shook his head in disgust. "Stupid fucker. I don't even know why we're bothering. Get your head out of your ass and get with the program, Reigler. Do you want your wife back or not?"

"It's not that easy—"

"That's not an answer." Daryl propped his hip on the edge of Jonathan's desk, folded his arms across his broad chest, and stared down at him.

"I told you—"

"You haven't told us shit, except to make excuses. Do you want to do this or not?"

"I—"

"You only have two options for an answer: yes or no. Which is it?"

Jonathan bit back a curse and shook his head. What the fuck? They knew his answer. Why was Daryl fucking pushing?

He reached for the cup of coffee and took a long swallow of the strong brew. It was nothing more than a stalling tactic and both his buddies knew it. Jonathan blew out a heavy sigh, his gaze focused on the worn paneling covering the far wall.

"Yes."

"Fine. Then I need both of you clowns to head down to the Blades' office at zero-nine-hundred tomorrow." Daryl shifted and pulled something from the side pocket of his cargo pants. He unfolded it, his brows lowering over his pale eyes as he skimmed it before shaking his head. A hint of a smile played around his mouth as he shook his head again.

Jonathan exchanged a questioning glance with Mac. "Why the fuck are we going down there? And what the fuck is so funny?"

Daryl pushed away from the desk as he tossed the sheet of paper at Jonathan. "Apparently the owner of the Blades is looking to hire a security firm to cover their games. I'm figuring this would be a great job for Cover Six Security until other shit starts rolling in."

Jonathan didn't bother to hide his confusion. Why the fuck would a hockey team need the kind of security they provided? He glanced at the paper, frowning as he read it.

And read it again, just in case he was missing something.

He wasn't.

"Are you out of your fucking mind? This isn't for us. This is for—"

"You want an in or not?"

Mac kicked out with one foot and sent his desk chair rolling across the floor. He snatched the paper from Jonathan's hands to read it for himself. The expression of disbelief that crossed his face matched Jonathan's.

"You have got to be fucking kidding me. They're looking for mall cops, not a personal security group."

"We all have to start somewhere."

"But—"

"Hey, it's up to you. If you want your in, there it is." Daryl grabbed his coffee and stepped away from the desk. "If you want it, be there at oh-nine-hundred. If not, don't show up. It's up to you."

"Where are you going to be?"

"I'm heading down to DC first thing in the morning for meetings." Daryl paused outside his office door and leveled Jonathan with a meaningful look. "Shit's about to take off, so I wouldn't waste too much time deciding."

Jonathan grabbed the paper from Mac and looked at it again, his fingers tightening around the edge and creasing it. As far as ideas went, this one ranked right up there in stupid-land. There wasn't even a guarantee this would get him closer to Sammie. In the same building, yeah, but anything other than that? Probably not.

Was it better than nothing? Yes.

Would it work? Doubtful.

Was Jonathan willing to toss a chance, no matter how slim, out the window? No way in hell.

He nodded in Daryl's direction then passed the paper to Mac. "Looks like we have an interview tomorrow morning."

"Well fuck."

chapter
SEVEN

They were coming off the ice from warm-ups when Sammie nearly tripped and fell because someone knocked into her from behind. She caught herself at the last minute then turned and shot at scowl at Shannon.

"What was that for?"

An identical scowl creased Shannon's face but it wasn't directed at Sammie—it was directed to someone in the stands. The goalie pushed Sammie again, urging her forward.

"I think you have a stalker."

"What? What are you talking about?"

"I just saw the guy from the bar last weekend."

"What? Where?" Sammie's heart skipped a beat then raced inside her chest. She tried to look around, wondering what Shannon was talking about, unable to dismiss the brief slice of—not fear, not exactly, but something close—that sent a chill scraping down her back. But she couldn't see anything because Shannon kept pushing at her until they were in the locker room.

"Are you sure you weren't seeing things?"

Shannon pushed the helmet up on her head and gave Sammie a look that silently asked if she was crazy. "Um, hello? This is me we're talking about. I don't *see things*."

Taylor and Dani stopped next to them. Dani's gaze slid from Shannon to Sammie and back again. "Don't see what? What aren't you seeing?"

"Reigs has a stalker."

"What?"

"I do not. You're just imagining things." Sammie put more strength into the words than she felt and forced a smile to her face. She didn't want to believe Shannon. The idea was too…too ludicrous. Unbelievable. Silly. She didn't have a stalker. Why would she? She wasn't anyone special, she didn't do anything to garner attention. She taught *kindergarten*, for crying out loud!

"I know what I saw, and I'm telling you, it's the same guy that was watching you at the bar last weekend."

"But that doesn't make sense. It can't be the same guy. He wouldn't even know where to find me." And crappola, now *she* was talking like a fool. She shook her head and made her way over to the bench, hoping to just sit and relax, get her mind on the game for the next few minutes before they headed back to the ice. Her teammates had other ideas because they joined her, crowding around her with varying expressions of curiosity and concern on their faces.

Taylor dropped to the bench beside her. "He might, if he saw that article this week."

"Somehow I doubt that." But another shiver danced across her flushed skin, chilling her. There had been nothing wrong with the article, and Sammie was actually proud of it, proud of the way it had portrayed the team in such a positive light, proud at how TR had focused on the strengths and challenges without making all of them sound like a bunch of whiny, wimpy little girls.

But there was no denying that the article had definitely brought some unwanted attention to her. Well, maybe that was exaggerating things a bit. Some of the faculty at the school had commented on it, teasing her a little, but mostly it had been all positive. Except for Chris Godfrey—and all he had done was start asking her out again, with maybe a little more determination than he had before.

"Shannon, are you positive it's the same guy?"

"Um, yeah. What the fuck? Of course, I'm positive. There's no way I'd confuse him with anyone else."

Taylor turned back to Sammie, a frown creasing her forehead. "Maybe I should say something to Chuckie. They just hired that security team for the games so maybe—"

"No. Absolutely not. Good grief. I don't have a stalker, so just stop. And even if I did, it's not like those goofy mall cops would be able to do anything about it. And seriously, why did Mr. Murphy even hire them? It's not like we need them—not when there isn't even a crowd."

Taylor pulled her lower lip between her teeth then looked away with a sigh. This was a sore subject for all of them: the lack of a crowd, low ticket sales, the constant worry that the newly-formed league wouldn't last.

At least they'd made it past four games. That had to say something, right? Because a few weeks ago, everyone had been convinced the rumors were right and that the league was going to fold before the fourth game.

"It looks like it's a bigger crowd this afternoon. That has to be a good sign, right?"

Everyone turned toward Dani and stared. A small flush crept along her cheekbones, making the freckles scattered across her fair skin stand out. "What? Stop looking at me like that. I'm trying to stay positive, okay?"

"Yeah, sure." Shannon rolled her eyes. "Now back to your stalker—"

"I don't have a stalker." Sammie pushed to her feet and grabbed her stick. "And I think Dani is right. The crowd does look a little bigger tonight. Has Chuckie said anything?"

"Not really, no." Taylor grabbed her own stick then hooked it behind her neck, twisting from side to side. "But he seems a little more upbeat about the way things are going."

Shannon laughed and tapped Taylor on the leg. "That's only because he's getting laid on a regular basis now."

"You did not just say that."

"Of course I did. Do you expect anything less from me?"

"Okay, enough. No more talk of stalkers or ticket sales or—or—or Taylor getting lucky. We have more important things to worry about."

"You're just jealous, Reigs. Admit it."

"No. I'm not." Sammie bit the inside of her cheek

to keep from smiling. The effort was wasted. "Well, okay. Maybe a little. Are you going to say you're not?"

"Ooo, *zing*." Shannon grabbed her chest and stumbled backward, a broad smile on her face. "Hit me where it hurts the most."

The three of them laughed at Shannon's antics, then quickly muffled their laughter when Coach Reynolds called for everyone's attention. A few minutes later, after being properly pumped-up, they headed back out to the ice to do their best to beat Philly.

At least, Sammie hoped they'd beat Philly. This was already their second time meeting the team on the ice, and the Blades had been soundly throttled the first time. They needed this win.

And she needed to stop being so pessimistic.

Sammie slid into position, slightly crouched, legs bent, the blade of her stick against the ice. The puck dropped, and action exploded around them as the Blades took possession. Taylor zipped to the right and took off, trying to get clear of Philly's D. But she was boxed in, unable to move past them.

Taylor glanced behind her then shot the puck between her legs, passing it to Sydney Stevens. One of the Philly players reached it first, spinning around to take it back.

Sammie crouched low and raced forward, her legs pumping as she sped across the ice. And crappola, she wasn't going to get to the net in time, not even close. And how the heck had that happened?

No. She wouldn't let it happen. Not this soon in the game. She crouched lower, increasing her speed as the Blades' other defenseman, Heather Witten, caught up. She could see Shannon in the net, getting into position to block the shot.

Sammie lunged, just like she had done last week. But her timing was off, she had moved too soon, before the Philly player had even pulled back to shoot. Sammie's shoulder caught the player in the chest, and they both went sprawling to the ice. Sammie rolled to her stomach, swept her stick across the ice and shot the puck behind her, away from Shannon, then scrambled to her feet.

Something hit her from behind and nearly sent her flying again. She regained her balance then spun around, frowning at the Philly player standing there, braced for a fight.

"Come on, let's go."

"What?"

"You heard me. Let's go." The other woman dropped her gloves to the ice with a wink. Sammie glanced around, frowning in confusion.

"We're not supposed to—"

"You really care about the rules?"

"But—" Sammie never finished because the other woman took a swing at her, catching her on the chin. It wasn't a hard hit, not even close, but her jaw was still sore from last week and it hurt. Not enough to bring tears to her eyes but enough to make her wince.

Sammie hesitated, but only for a brief second. Then she tossed her own stick and gloves to the ice and swung out with her fist. Once, twice. Once more. Not hard, not even close—Sammie knew nothing about fighting, only what she'd seen on television. But they weren't *really* fighting. At least, she didn't think so. This was just for show.

Wasn't it?

The other woman's fist caught her in the mouth,

hard enough that Sammie started to wonder if maybe she had been wrong and this *was* a real fight. She tasted the bitter metallic tang of blood then clenched her jaw and drove her head into the other woman's chest, reaching around her to grab the hem of her jersey. They kept scuffling, arms and fists flying and occasionally connecting until Sammie finally pulled the jersey over the woman's head and pushed her down.

The shrill blast of a whistle finally registered and she turned to see the officials motioning to them—to *her*. Sammie blinked, surprised at the cheers and applause echoing around them. Her gaze darted around the ice, noticing the smiles on her teammates' faces—and on the faces of the Philly players as well.

Well, crappola. Maybe they should have done this a few games ago if people were going to get so excited about it.

Sammie straightened her jersey then leaned over, offering the other woman a hand up before collecting her gear from the ice.

"Not bad, short stuff."

"Thanks. I've never done that before."

"First time for everything, right?" The other woman laughed then grabbed her own gear. Sammie started skating back to the bench but was stopped when someone tugged on her arm. She turned, surprised to see the ref glaring at her.

"Wrong way, 88. In the box. Both of you."

Sammie bit back a smile then skated over to the penalty box, her stick raised high at the continuing cheers. She shouldn't be smiling, she knew that. And she'd probably get in trouble later—they weren't supposed to be fighting or hitting or body checking or anything like that. That was a big no-no. But it had been fun—not that Sammie would admit that out loud. Well, okay, yes she would. To her teammates at least. And the crowd had obviously enjoyed it.

Her gaze scanned the crowd, still cheering and clapping as she stepped into the penalty box. Then something caught her eye and the smile died on her face. She tripped and nearly fell, too stunned to do anything more than stumble to the bench, her gaze still focused on the single face standing by the glass.

Still focused on that intent, dark gaze looking back at her. Concern, laughter, pride, worry. She saw all of that and more in the space of a frantic heartbeat.

It couldn't be. She had to be seeing things.

But she wasn't. And there was no mistaking those eyes, that face. Not when he was standing less than twenty feet away, watching her.

Jon.

chapter
EIGHT

Sammie had never been so furious before. Upset, yes. Frustrated, absolutely. Angry, sure. But this...this *rage* that was running through her veins was something new. Potent. Powerful. Searing.

She'd heard the phrase *seeing red* before, had always laughed at it as nothing more than a colorful cliché—but it was true. Oh, so true. She really was seeing red, her vision clouded by a dark mist that colored everything—including all reason.

She'd drawn a handful of penalties throughout the game, the total minutes exceeding those of every single combined penalty minutes she'd ever had before. It was a new personal record. Not one that she was proud of, and one that had Coach Reynolds chewing her out. Repeatedly.

Any other time, Sammie would have been mortified at being the subject of the coach's ire. Would have been humiliated at the idea that she'd let her team down.

Not that anyone other than Coach Reynolds seemed to be upset by her performance. Her teammates had congratulated her, tapped her on the legs and arms with their sticks every single time she came out of the box—like they were proud of her for some reason.

Any other time, she would have berated herself for causing the Blades to lose—and their loss *was* her fault. Philly had scored on the power play during her last stint in the bin, putting them ahead by one point.

It turned out to be the game-winning goal.

Yes, at any other time, Sammie would be beating herself up over it. But not now. Not tonight. She was too furious to care—about the loss, about disappointing her teammates, about her own dismal performance or the verbal set-down Coach Reynolds had given her.

The only thing she cared about was the man she had seen watching her during the game, with those dark, haunted eyes focused solely on her. Sammie wanted to run out of the locker room and track him down, confront him. Cross-check him then slam him into the boards.

It was the urge to do violence that finally cut through the fury boiling her blood. Sammie wasn't violent. She never had been. This urge, this anger, was new to her. Too new. Too confusing.

Too overwhelming.

She closed her eyes, took a deep breath, and let it out slowly, like she had seen Shannon do a hundred times before in preparation for a game. Maybe there was a trick she didn't know about, or something else she needed to do besides take deep breaths, because it wasn't working. Instead of finding an elusive calm, all she was doing was making herself lightheaded.

She sensed someone sitting beside her. No, make that two someones—one person on each side. Sammie inhaled again, long and deep, and tried to pretend she was alone.

"What are you doing?"

Sammie shook her head, silently telling Taylor to go away. Her friend didn't move, so Sammie released the breath with a long sigh and sucked in another one, deeper this time.

"Are you trying to make yourself pass out?"

The question came from her right—Shannon, her voice filled with just a hint of laughter.

Sammie shook her head again, released her breath, pulled in another. Again. Once more. Something nudged her in the side—hard—and she exhaled with a small grunt before opening her eyes and shooting a glare in Shannon's direction.

"Leave me alone. I'm trying to calm myself down."

Shannon's brows shot up in disbelief. "By hyperventilating?"

"I'm not hyperventilating. I'm doing deep-breathing exercises." Sammie forced the words from between clenched teeth then pushed to her feet. The room spun and strange little dots flashed in front of her eyes. She blinked and dropped back to the bench.

"Yup. Hyperventilating." Shannon muttered something else then placed her hand on the back of Sammie's head and pushed her forward so hard, Sammie smacked her nose against her knee.

"Ouch! What are you doing?" She pushed against Shannon's hold and sat up. "I'm not hyperventilating. Just leave me alone, okay?"

Taylor's hand closed around her arm, holding her in place when she tried to stand again. "Are you going to tell us what the hell happened out there? It was like you were possessed or something."

"Not necessarily in a bad way. I mean, I know Coach wasn't happy but damn, girl, you were unfuckingbelievable out there." Shannon offered her an angelic smile then ruined the effect by nudging Sammie in the side so hard she jostled against Taylor.

"Nothing happened."

Both women snorted their disbelief. Sammie rolled her eyes, grabbed her bag off the floor, then pushed to her feet once more. Shannon and Taylor fell into step beside her, like they were her own personal bodyguards.

Sammie almost snorted. Bodyguards? Not likely. More like they were intent on getting answers and wouldn't leave until she gave them some.

"Guys, I'm serious. Nothing happened. And I'm not talking about it."

"Which means something *did* happen." Taylor pushed through the locker room door, turning to the side as she held it open. Shannon nudged Sammie through then darted in front of her, walking backward with a grin on her face.

"And you know us. You're not leaving until you tell us."

"There's nothing to tell." Sammie tried stepping around Shannon but the other woman simply moved in front of her, stopping her. And Taylor was right there with her, effectively blocking her escape.

She knew they meant well, that they were worried about her despite the teasing laughter. But she didn't want to talk about it. Not now, not when the anger and fury were still so close to the surface. Not when talking about it would open wounds she had no desire to acknowledge.

And not when she was so afraid that her anger was nothing more than camouflage for deeper feelings she had thought long dead and buried.

Sammie adjusted the grip on her bag and tossed it over her shoulder then forced a smile to her face. "Guys, seriously. There's nothing to talk about. All I want to do is get home. It's already late."

She motioned around the rink with a nod of her head. It *was* late—the Philly team was already on their way back home; the crowd was gone, leaving nothing behind except the ghostly echoes of cheers and jeers. Even the majority of her teammates were gone, already on their way home instead of heading out like they usually did after each game. The Thanksgiving break was coming up, meaning they had off for the next week. Some of her teammates were heading home, to Boston and Maine and Minnesota.

And that's where Sammie wanted to go: home. To spend time with Clare in front of the fire, reading stories or playing dolls before her daughter's bedtime.

But Shannon merely shook her head, determination glinting in her eyes. "It's not that late. It's not even six yet. We should go out and talk—"

"No. I don't want to go out. I want to get home and spend time with Clare. Okay?" Sammie pushed by Shannon, her steps quickening as her two teammates followed her. The frustration that had been simmering in her chest the last few minutes came dangerously close to exploding, surprising her. Sammie's steps faltered as she fought the urge to kick and scream and hit. What was with her? Why was she so angry?

She knew why. But why was she so dangerously close to taking it out on her friends? This wasn't like her, not even close. Maybe she should tell them, just to get everything off her chest. Maybe that would help, like some kind of therapeutic cleansing.

No, she couldn't. She *wouldn't*. They'd ask questions. Lots of questions. Questions she didn't feel like answering because it would be too painful. And God, she didn't want to drag everything to the surface again. She was past that. Or she thought she had been—until seeing Jon last weekend.

Until seeing him tonight.

Why? Why was here? What did he want? It had taken her eighteen months to get over him. To forget about him. To forget about what he'd done and how much he'd hurt her.

Except she had never truly forgotten. Not really. She didn't think she ever would. Not because of Clare—their daughter was the single ray of hope that she always clung to. No, she was afraid she'd never truly forget because she still *felt* too much—and she probably always would.

What kind of pathetic statement did that make about her and her life?

No, she couldn't tell her friends, no matter how much she might want to. If she did, she'd end up admitting things she didn't want to admit. Things she'd prefer would just go away to wither and die so she could finally move on.

Sammie blew out another breath, trying to release some of the frustration that kept building inside her. She readjusted her grip on the gear bag and tried to force another smile as she turned toward Shannon and Taylor. "Listen, maybe we can get together next weekend or something and—"

Her words died, morphing into a small grunt when Shannon abruptly pushed her to the side. No, not to the side—behind her. Like the goalie was suddenly playing bodyguard. The bag dropped from Sammie's shoulder and hit the floor with a heavy thud, the sound oddly loud in the charged silence.

"What the hell?" Taylor muttered the confused phrase, echoing Sammie's own thoughts. "Shannon—"

"Okay, buddy. I'm tired of this bullshit. Who the fuck are you?"

Sammie glanced at Taylor then pushed around Shannon, trying to see who she was talking to. Shannon grabbed her arm and tugged, trying to pull her behind her again. It didn't work. Sammie's feet were glued to the floor, dread and fear and surprise and a hundred other different things holding her immobile.

But she shouldn't be surprised, not really. She knew he was here—she'd seen him herself earlier, knew he was at the game. But why was he still here? There was no reason for him to be here.

The anger and fury that had been building all night finally exploded, unleashing something primitive inside her. Maybe it was just a need for revenge. Or maybe it was just simply a need to hurt him as much as he had hurt her. Sammie didn't know, and at that precise moment, she didn't care.

She simply curled her fists and lunged toward Jon.

chapter NINE

This is bullshit. Who the fuck are you?

Jon blinked, trying to process the words—he hadn't been expecting that kind of language, especially not from the blonde who looked like she should be on the cover of some beauty magazine. It was the incongruity of the words coming from that full, pouty mouth that left him stunned and unable to react.

At least, that's what he told himself. It was better than acknowledging he'd been totally caught off-guard by the petite brunette with a mop of wild curls who was suddenly wailing on him with both fists.

Maybe *wailing* was an exaggeration.

Sammie got in two wild hits against his chest, the contact barely registering because they were so ineffective. He stepped back—more to get out of her way than to protect himself, just in case she actually got lucky. She kept swinging, though, her small fists slicing through the air in a wild frenzy as she muttered under her breath.

He stood still, not sure what to do. Move closer and let her hit him? Would that settle her down? Make her feel better?

Some inner instinct told him it wouldn't. Whatever rage was propelling Sammie wouldn't be satisfied by hitting him. This was something bigger. Something deeper. Something that had been building for a long time.

For two years and three months. Maybe longer.

Maybe he *should* let her hit him. Just let her pound on him until she got it out of her system, until she felt better. If he thought it would work, he'd do exactly that. But he knew Sammie, knew this wasn't like her. Sammie didn't have a violent bone in her body.

He stepped forward, reaching out to catch her fists with his hands before she accidentally hurt herself. She took another wild swing, this one clipping him under the chin hard enough to make his teeth snap together.

"Fuck!"

Jon blinked as the single word split the silence of the chilled air. He'd been thinking that exact same word, had been ready to utter it himself, but it hadn't come from him.

It had come from Sammie. From sweet, mild, innocent Sammie, who never, ever swore.

Maybe he didn't know her as well as he thought he had. Maybe the passing of time had changed her as much as it had changed him.

Sammie's mouth snapped shut, her eyes widening in surprise as she clutched her hand in front of her. Her teammates hurried to her side, flanking her. The blonde draped an arm around her shoulders and laughed.

"Whoa. Reigs. Damn. My ears are burning." The words sounded right, carrying just enough humor. Jon didn't miss the hint of ice underlying them, though. And he certainly didn't miss the clear threat that flashed in the blonde's brown eyes when their gazes met.

Sammie muttered something under her breath, the words too low for him to make out. She released the hold on her hand then shook it in front of her, glaring at him through narrowed eyes.

Jonathan stepped forward then abruptly stopped and jammed his hands into the back pockets of his cargo pants. "You okay?"

"Don't talk to me! Just—just go away!"

The two women exchanged a silent glance then stepped closer to Sammie, angling their bodies so they were in front of her. Jonathan recognized the move for what it was: they were protecting Sammie, silently telling him he'd have to go through them to get to her.

He ignored the silent warning and moved forward another step. "Sammie, are you okay?"

A frown creased the blonde's face as she darted a glance first at him then at Sammie. "Wait. You two know each other?"

"Yes."

"No." Sammie's loud answer almost drowned out his own, earning a frown from her two friends. He took another step forward.

"Sammie—"

"Go away, Jon." He saw the way her throat worked, how she seemed to struggle to get the words out as she blinked, not quite looking at him. Pain lodged in his chest, a heavy ache that grew with each breath he struggled to pull in. He pushed it back, ruthlessly ignoring it.

Just as he ignored the pain flashing in Sammie's eyes.

At least, he tried to. He failed at both.

What the fuck was he doing here? Why was he so determined to see Sammie, to talk to her, after what he'd done? He had no right to do either, not after everything he'd put her through. He'd given up that right when he walked away without a word.

But he couldn't make himself walk away now, no matter how futile he knew this was. He needed to at least *try*. But try *what*? He didn't know, not yet.

Talk to her? Try to explain? Try to make her understand?

Apologize?

Yes, definitely. Not that he expected her to ever forgive him. Hell, he couldn't forgive himself. Why should he expect anything different from her? He didn't. So maybe this was nothing more than a pathetic, last-ditch effort to find absolution, to make himself feel better.

Which was nothing but utter fucking bullshit. He didn't want absolution. Fuck, he didn't deserve it, not after everything he'd done.

What he wanted was his wife back.

Yeah, he could just imagine her reaction if he told her that, especially with the way she was standing there, glaring at him as she tried so hard to hide the pain he had caused.

What the fuck was he doing? He should just leave her alone. Walk away and let her get on with her life. She didn't want him there, that much was obvious from just looking at her. And she sure as hell didn't need him—she had moved on, creating a new life without him.

So why the fuck was he still standing there?

Because he couldn't walk away. Not again. Not without at least trying.

Jonathan released a sharp sigh, his gaze moving over the three women watching him. The blonde narrowed her own eyes and he half-expected her to lunge at him and take over where Sammie had left off. Something told him that her punches would be a hell of a lot more substantial than Sammie's.

"So who the hell are you?"

The question was directed at him, not at Sammie, but she didn't hesitate to answer.

"Nobody. He's nobody."

Had he expected anything different? No, not really. Jonathan caught her gaze, held it for a few heartbreaking seconds, then looked at her teammates.

"I'm Jonathan Reigler. Sammie's husband."

You'd think he had just announced that the building was ready to explode from their reactions. Stunned disbelief gave way to angry exclamations, the exact words lost in the combined shouts of Sammie's teammates—and from Sammie herself. He didn't miss the silent accusation on Sammie's face, didn't miss the way her eyes narrowed as she shook her head and took a step back.

The other two women were giving him their own dirty looks, the expressions holding more than a hint of confusion as they studied him.

"You're her ex?"

Jonathan mentally winced at the sharpness of the other woman's voice—not the blonde, but the one with the odd amber-colored eyes. He didn't have a chance to respond—not that he had really planned on it, since there was nothing to respond to—before the blonde stepped forward and pointed an accusing finger at his chest.

"You're the one who's been following her. I saw you at the bar last weekend. You were watching her."

"I—"

"Don't fucking deny it. I saw you."

Jonathan clenched his teeth, felt the muscle jump in his jaw. "I was there. Yes."

"What are you, some kind of fucking stalker?"

"I—" Jonathan snapped his jaw shut. He'd been ready to deny it when the realization hit him. Yeah, he had been stalking Sammie. Not deliberately, not in that sense—and certainly not with sinister intentions. But the woman in front of him wouldn't believe that so he kept his mouth shut and simply stared at her. Any other person would have backed away under that stare, their sense of self-preservation kicking in. But not the blonde. Instead of running away, she actually moved closer and returned the stare, not giving an inch.

Unwelcome admiration flashed through him. She had balls, he had to give her that. And he honestly wasn't sure who would have backed down first if Sammie's other teammate hadn't pulled the blonde away.

"Shannon, don't start."

"I'm not—"

"Yes, you are. Now's not the time." Whiskey-eyes leveled her own stare at him, one that sized him up then quickly dismissed him, the way someone would dismiss a discarded piece of windblown trash tumbling through an abandoned parking lot.

He ignored both women and focused instead on

Sammie, who was still standing there, watching him with wide brown eyes.

"Can we talk?"

She shook her head, causing a few curls to fall into her eye. "I don't think—"

"Ten minutes. That's all." *For now.* He glanced at her teammates. "They can wait for you."

Sammie chewed on her lower lip, her gaze darting from him to the two women and back again. She turned her head, looking behind her, then released a heavy sigh. The sound was filled with resignation—and with doubt.

"Ten minutes. And Shannon and Taylor stay here."

"Sammie, I don't think—"

Sammie waved her hand, interrupting the blonde. "It's only ten minutes. And we'll be right over there."

She pointed to the closest row of seats, ten yards away, then started walking toward them. Jonathan hesitated then started following her. He had hoped for a little more privacy but he wasn't in a position to be picky. Hell, he wasn't in any position, period.

Sammie came to a stop near the end row of seats then turned to face him. She folded her arms in front of her as her chin edged up a notch. Stubborn. Determined. Maybe even a little impatient. But he didn't miss the wariness in her deep brown eyes, or the flash of pain.

He hesitated, not sure if he should stand or sit. Sit, he decided. It might put her a little more at ease, if he wasn't standing there, towering over her.

Silence stretched around them, sharp and uncomfortable. And fuck, now what? He had no idea what to say, where to start. He hadn't planned this through, and he sure as hell hadn't counted on an audience. He glanced behind him and yes, sure enough, her teammates hadn't moved. The two women stood there, watching them, no doubt ready to rush to Sammie's defense.

Jonathan turned back and flashed a small smile at Sammie. "Your friends look like they're ready to tear my head off."

"Stop it, Jon. You didn't come here to talk about my teammates."

"You're right. I didn't. I—"

"Have you been following me? Stalking me, like Shannon said?"

"No." Jonathan shifted on the hard seat and looked away. "Not like that. I—I *was* at the bar last weekend, yes. But I—" He stopped, cleared his throat, met her gaze for a second and quickly looked away. "I wasn't stalking you. I just wanted to see you."

"Why?"

"Because I—" He stopped, the words he wanted—*needed*—to say refusing to come out. He took a deep breath and forced himself to meet Sammie's questioning gaze. "I wanted to see you. To explain. To apologize—"

"It's too late for that, Jon. I told you that last weekend at the house."

"Yeah, I know you did. But you deserve to hear why."

"Really?" She tilted her head to the side and stared at him. "Don't you think you should have thought of that over two years ago?"

"Yeah, I should have. But where I was—" He looked away and cleared his throat. Fuck, what was wrong with him? Why couldn't he just tell her? He'd been so fucked up, convinced he was a monster. Convinced the best thing he could do was let her go. To let her find happiness with someone who deserved her.

Yeah, he'd been so totally fucked in the head back then. But how could he tell her that without sounding weak and whiny?

He ran a hand down his face, felt the stubble prick his palm, heard it rasp in the chilled silence. "Sammie—"

"Why, Jon? Why are you here? Why now? What do you want?"

I want my family back. You. Clare. The three of us.

The confession echoed in his head, over and over. But fuck, he couldn't tell her that. Not yet. She'd laugh in his face, or worse—and he would deserve all of it and more.

"I just want to talk. That's all. You deserve the truth." He pushed to his feet, the motion bringing him within inches of Sammie, close enough he could feel the heat of anger and smell the faintest hint of whatever shampoo she had used. He expected her to take a step back, to put distance between them, but she didn't. Was this her way of standing up to him? Or did she feel it too, the invisible pull that still existed between them? It would be so easy to close the physical distance, to pull her into his arms and hold her and wish the past away.

And probably get his ass kicked in the process.

"All I want is to talk, Sammie. That's it. After that, if you tell me to go to hell, I will. But here isn't the place, not with your friends ready to come over here and tear me apart."

"I don't think—"

"I know. I wouldn't want anything to do with me, either. Not after what I did. But I'm still asking for this chance to talk."

"It won't change anything, Jon. I've moved on. We both have."

He didn't miss the way her eyes narrowed when she said *we*, didn't miss the cold accusation in her voice. She wasn't talking about the two of them—she was talking about her and Clare.

He ignored the pain that sliced through him, swallowed the urge to ask about his daughter. He couldn't, not yet. He wasn't ready, was afraid that just saying Clare's name out loud would reduce him to a quivering sack of spineless jelly. But fuck, it had to be killing Sammie, she had to be wondering *why* he hadn't said anything, why he hadn't asked about his daughter.

He needed to tell her. Had to force himself to admit his biggest fear. But not here, not with an audience.

"Wednesday evening. When you get off work."

Sammie frowned and stepped back, finally putting distance between them. "What?"

"Meet me Wednesday after work. Just to talk."

"You can talk now."

"No, I can't. Not with an audience. Not with a time limit."

"That's not a good idea."

"You're right, it's probably not. But I'm asking you anyway."

"Jon—"

"At the upper level of the town center. The parking lot by the movie theater."

"I—"

"Seventeen hundred—five o'clock. Just to talk."

"Jon—"

"Wednesday. Five o'clock."

He reached out, ran his hand along her arm to her wrist, then stepped back. He didn't miss the way her body stiffened, didn't miss the way her eyes flared in surprise.

And he sure as hell didn't miss the soft intake of surprised breath or the way the pulse beat in her throat sped up. Anger? Maybe. But maybe there was more to it than that.

He turned and headed for the exit, moving past the other two women with a quick nod of acknowledgment. He heard them swear under their breath, heard the sound of their steps as they hurried toward Sammie.

No doubt to make sure she was okay.

Would she tell them he had asked to meet her on Wednesday?

Probably.

Would they try to talk her out of it?

Definitely.

Would she listen to them?

Fuck, he hoped not. But it was a chance he had to take.

Chapter TEN

Sammie had been distracted all day, which was fair enough, she supposed, since all of her kids had been just as distracted. She'd done her best to keep them focused, to keep them on task throughout the day, but her mind was too focused on the clock.

She glanced at it now then pressed the flat of her hand against her stomach, trying to stop the odd quivering that had grown worse with each passing hour. It was almost three-thirty now. In a little more than ninety minutes, she'd be meeting Jon.

Maybe.

She hadn't made her mind up yet. In fact, she had tried to convince herself that she wasn't going to go. She had no desire to meet him, no desire to hear what he had to say. She owed him exactly nothing. And there wasn't anything he could say, no excuse he could give, to erase the pain she still felt.

So why was she still looking at the clock, watching

the minutes tick away?

She knew why and called herself a fool. She was going to meet him, no matter how much she tried to convince herself otherwise, because some perverted part of her wanted to hear what he had to say. What excuse would he give her for throwing away their marriage, for tossing her and Clare to the side?

The pain was still sharp, brutal, even after all this time. God, she was such a fool. He shouldn't hold the power to still hurt her, not after everything that had happened. But he did, and she was very much afraid of what that meant.

She opened her eyes and tried to push all thoughts of Jon from her mind. She wouldn't go. She couldn't. It was too late. Whatever he wanted to say, whatever excuses he thought to make, couldn't matter.

She repeated the words to herself as she moved around the room, straightening the small chairs, picking up the stray toy here and a forgotten book there, things that never seemed to make their way back to the shelf. She moved to the chalkboard, mindlessly erasing the simple spelling words she had so carefully printed in big block letters on the black surface earlier.

If only she could erase the memories just as easily.

A knock echoed in the quiet room and she looked up, startled at the noise. Chris Godfrey lounged against the doorframe, the tie loose around his neck, the top button of his collar undone. A worn leather briefcase dangled from his right hand, his blue eyes shining with amusement as he watched her.

"I figured you would have been gone already."

Sammie offered him a small smile as she replaced the eraser then dusted the chalk from her hands. "I'm getting there. Just wanted to finish cleaning up first."

His gaze darted around the neat room. One pale brow lifted in silent amusement. "Looks clean to me."

"Yes, well, you should have seen it twenty minutes ago. Not so much."

Chris laughed, the sound cheerful and mellow and unthreatening. He taught second-grade math and had the patience of a saint and the friendly disposition of a loyal pet. Just an inch or so under six feet, with carefully trimmed blonde hair and laughing blue eyes. Friendly. Unassuming. Always neatly dressed in khakis and a button-down shirt and brown leather loafers.

Those blue eyes watched her now, quietly assessing. Sammie turned away and grabbed her coat, holding her breath and hoping that he wouldn't—

"Did you want to grab a coffee or anything before heading home?"

She released her breath with a mental wince and turned to face him, a small, apologetic smile on her face. "I can't, not today. Too much to do."

How many times had he asked her out? For coffee. A quick bite to eat. Nothing threatening, nothing serious. How many times had she said no?

Every single time.

She looked at him now, watching as he quickly hid the disappointment at her answer, and wondered why he kept asking.

And wondered why she always said no. Chris was friendly. Attractive. Even-tempered and good-natured.

Safe.

But she still said no. Every single time.

The reason why slammed into her and nearly knocked her off her feet. It wasn't because he was a co-worker. It wasn't because she simply wasn't interested—in him *or* in a relationship.

It was because he wasn't Jon.

And oh God, had she really been comparing him to her ex-husband all this time? Comparing him—and finding him falling far short?

He was nothing like Jon. Jon was tall, broad in the shoulders and chest, all hard planes and sharp angles. His body had been chiseled and sculpted from years of tossing hay bales and working with his family's small herd of cattle, and later from his time in the military. Jon had rugged features: a wide jaw covered in perpetual stubble no matter how often he shaved and deep-set eyes that could freeze you in place or melt your heart, depending on what he wanted.

Jon wasn't *safe*. He never had been.

Chris was almost the exact opposite. Too laid-back. Too relaxed. Too even-keeled. Like a cocker spaniel, who would curl by your side and patiently wait, grateful for whatever tiny bit of attention you would give him.

Jon was—he was like a pit bull. He didn't patiently wait for anything, he demanded, settling for nothing less than your undivided attention. And he'd be right there beside you in a fight, standing there and guarding your back, defending you until the very end.

Everyone except her. With her, Jon had simply walked away without a word.

Only that wasn't like him. That wasn't something he would do. Not unless he had a reason.

And oh God, why was she making excuses for him? Why now, after all this time?

Because—

No, there was no *because*. There couldn't be. She wouldn't—*couldn't*—allow it.

Except she was afraid she already had.

Sammie swallowed back a groan of frustration and anger and pain, worried that it would end in a scream of self-pity and sorrow if she let it out. Afraid it wouldn't stop at all. Maybe she wasn't as successful as she thought because Chris's brows shot up in surprise and he pushed away from the doorframe.

"Are you okay?"

"Yes. Fine." Except she wasn't, and hadn't been in a long time. She jammed her arms into the sleeves of her coat, grabbed the stuffed tote bag resting beside her desk, and hurried across the room. She almost plowed into Chris as she turned to pull the door closed behind her. He caught her arm to steady her then quickly dropped it and moved back.

She mumbled an apology then practically raced down the hall, the hem of her long skirt swirling around her ankles. She needed to get out of here, needed to go somewhere to think.

She yanked the straps of the tote bag over her shoulder and glanced at her watch. Was it too late? No, she still had a little more than an hour. That should be plenty of time.

Sammie pushed through the double doors and raced down the steps, one hand grasping the railing to steady herself as she pulled her cell phone from the tote bag with another and selected a number from her list of contacts.

The phone rang three times before a breathes voice answered. "Reigs. What's up?"

"I need you to stop me from making a huge mistake."

chapter ELEVEN

Jonathan circled the parking lot for the second time, the ball of dread that had taken up residence in his gut growing heavier. He hadn't realized the place would be so fucking crowded, not on a Wednesday evening, hadn't even given any thought to the fact that it was the day before Thanksgiving.

That was his fucking problem. He hadn't been thinking—he'd been dreaming, totally lost in a fantasy world of his own making.

He ground his teeth together and turned up the last aisle, his gaze moving from side-to-side, searching for Sammie's car. He could drive right by it and he probably wouldn't even realize it.

Fuck.

He should have planned better. Given her a specific location instead of just saying the parking lot. What a fucking idiot.

He shook his head at his own stupidity and turned

out of the aisle, heading to the far end of the lot for another pass-through. For all he knew, Sammie wasn't even here. And wouldn't that be something? He could spend all night driving around the parking lot, searching for her, while she was at home, eating dinner or watching television or reading or—

Or playing with their daughter.

He rubbed one fist against his chest, told himself to ignore the dull pain that settled there every time he thought of Clare. Fuck. If Mac and Daryl could see him now, they'd be laughing their fucking asses off. They already thought he was close to losing it, that he was dragging his feet and playing games instead of just jumping in and taking what he wanted. What the fuck did they know about it?

Not a damn thing.

And he was starting to think he didn't either.

He clenched his jaw, his back teeth grinding together again, and turned down the far aisle, the one closest to the center's upper-level plaza. There was only one row of cars here, all lined up on his left. What were the chances that Sammie would have lucked out and found a spot this close?

What were the chances of her even being here?

His gaze darted to the right, scanning the crowd of people coming and going. Couples. Families. Groups of teenagers. Laughing and talking, bundled against the cold evening air. Some of them moved toward the parking lot, while others made their way to the stores and restaurants on the upper level or headed toward the escalators and stairs leading to the lower level. A few people even sat on the benches scattered around the small plaza, taking a quick break or waiting—

Jonathan slammed on the brakes and threw the car into *Reverse*, backing up a few feet before hitting the brakes again. He ignored the impatient blaring of the horn coming from the car behind him as he hit the button for the passenger window to lower it.

No, he wasn't seeing things. There was Sammie, sitting on the bench, huddled in a jacket that looked more suited for Spring than Winter.

He leaned across the seat. "Sammie! Hey, Sammie!"

She looked up, her gaze moving along the line of cars backed up behind him before finally resting on him. For a second, Jonathan was afraid she'd ignore him, that she'd simply stand up and walk away.

She hesitated then pushed to her feet and swung a tote bag over her shoulder before making her way to his car. She was wearing a long skirt with some kind of abstract pattern on it, the hem swirling around the ankles of her boots. Her dark curls bounced around her face and she brushed them away with an impatient swipe of her hand before grabbing the door handle and pulling it open.

The car behind him hit the horn again, longer this time. Jonathan looked in the rearview mirror, ready to tell the driver to stick it up his ass. Sammie slammed the door closed and pointed over her shoulder.

"You're kind of holding up traffic."

Jonathan pursed his lips, swallowing back the words that had come so close to tumbling out, then started driving again. "I didn't think it would be this crowded."

"Well, it is the day before Thanksgiving."

"Um, yeah." He turned left, heading away from the crowd and traffic. Sammie stiffened next to him.

"Where are you going?"

Was that panic he heard in her voice? He glanced over, noticed the way her shoulders hunched around her ears and the way her chin tilted up.

"I'm just trying to find a place to park."

Her shoulders dropped a little, and he didn't miss the quick sigh of relief that spilled from her parted lips. His hands tightened on the wheel.

"Christ, Sammie. What the hell? Did you think I was going to kidnap you or something?"

"No. No, of course not."

He grunted but didn't say anything, didn't bother telling her that she didn't sound very convincing.

He finally found an empty spot, at the very far end of the lot, and maneuvered the car so he could back into it. Then he turned the engine off and sat there.

Silence filled the interior. Thick. Heavy. Oppressive. And fuck. Okay. Now what? Maybe he should start the engine again, just to turn on the radio for background music. No, music would be too distracting, would make it too hard to talk.

Not that there was any talking going on.

Jonathan wrapped both hands around the steering wheel, his grip so tight, he was surprised the damn thing didn't bend. He stared straight ahead, not knowing where to start.

"I—thank you for coming." And fuck, could he get any lamer?

Sammie shifted in the seat, looking out the window instead of at him. "I almost didn't. Shannon convinced me I should. She, uh, she said I needed to find out why. For closure."

"Closure." Jonathan repeated the word, dread sending ice through his veins. Was that why she was here, because she wanted *closure*? Wasn't that something you needed so you could move on? So you could put things behind you?

Fuck.

"Yeah. She said I wouldn't be able to move on without it."

"Closure?"

"Yes. She—"

"What is she, some kind of fucking shrink?" And fuck, he hadn't meant to say that out loud, hadn't meant for the words to sound so sharp. Sammie stiffened in the seat and watched him through narrowed eyes, her expression unreadable.

"This was a bad idea. I should go—"

"No, wait." He reached for her, let his hand drop to the console before he touched her. "Sammie, please. I just…"

She watched him, waiting for him to finish whatever he'd been ready to say. But he didn't know how to finish, wasn't sure what to say. He just…what?

He fucked up?

He was sorry for destroying what they had?

He was sorry for giving up?

Or maybe he should tell her he was nothing more than a fucking coward, afraid to face what he'd become.

Afraid for her to see what kind of monster he really was.

She shifted in the seat, anger clear on her face. But under the anger was something else: pain. Hurt. Betrayal. Each emotion cut through him, ripping open wounds he'd fought so long to ignore, wounds that had never healed.

"What do you want, Jon? Why are you here? Now,

after everything you did?"

"I—"

"Do you even know what you did to me? How much you hurt me?" Her voice broke and she looked away, her throat working as she swallowed. "And I never knew *why*. You couldn't even bother to tell me why. One day, everything was fine, and the next, I'm being served with divorce papers and told I need to move. That the only home my daughter—*our* daughter—ever knew was no longer her home."

She turned back to face him, her dark eyes filled with tears. His heart shattered into a million shards as a single tear fell and trailed down her cheek.

"I didn't know—"

"You didn't know?" She shouted the words at him, fury replacing the hurt that had been in her voice only seconds before. "How could you not know? Or was it that you didn't care? Why, Jon? That's all I want to know. Why? What was it that I did that was so awful that you divorced me while you were deployed? What did I do to make you turn your back on your own daughter?"

"It wasn't you—"

"Your own daughter, Jon! And you still haven't asked about her. Not once." Sammie dragged in a shaky breath and wiped at the tears trailing down her cheek. Anger flashed in her eyes again, brighter this time, as she leaned closer. "Do you even know how old she is? Do you even remember her name? Do you even care?"

Jonathan jerked back, the words more painful than any punch he'd ever taken. Sammie had every right to her anger, had every right to hurl the accusations at him, but they still hurt.

Fuck, they hurt.

And underneath the hurt was irrational anger—at Sammie. At himself. At the time he'd thrown away these last two years, convincing himself he was doing the right thing.

He swallowed past the misplaced anger, forced himself to meet Sammie's watery gaze, forced the words past the bitter lump in his throat. "Clare Margaret Reigler. She turned three last month, on the eighteenth."

If he had expected surprise from Sammie, he'd have been wrong. Fury flashed in her eyes a second before she swung her hand in his direction. Jonathan snagged her arm mid-air, stopping her before she could slap him.

"Damn you. Damn you, damn you, damn you!" She struggled against his hold, her voice breaking as tears coursed down her cheeks. He released her arm, waiting for her to take another swing at him, knowing he deserved that and so much more.

But she didn't swing at him. She didn't do anything except sit there, staring at something past his shoulder, her expression oddly vacant.

"Sammie—"

"Why, Jon? Why?" Her voice was hoarse and scratchy, barely more than a whisper. "You remember, but you couldn't be bothered to ask? To check and see how your own daughter was? To even acknowledge her? Why? To hate me is one thing but—"

"Hate? Sammie, I don't hate you—"

Her gaze darted to his for a brief second then slid away. "Don't you? Why else would you have done what you did?"

"Sammie—"

"To take it out on Clare—"

"I don't hate—"

"Then why? Why did you—"

"Fuck!" Jonathan shouted the word then slammed his fist against the steering wheel, hard enough to cause the horn to emit a pathetic squeal. "Because you deserved better than a monster!"

Sammie sat back, her teary-gaze wide as she stared at him. "I don't—"

"I'm a fucking monster, Sammie." His voice broke and he shook his head, turning away from her as he forced himself to calm down. He reminded himself that this was why he asked to see her—to tell her the truth. To tell her what he'd become.

And to hope she could find it somewhere in her to forgive him.

He ignored her questioning gaze, ignored the tears that clung to her lower lashes, forced himself to stare at his hands.

Large. Callused.

Stained with blood.

He curled one fist and rested it against his thigh, wrapped the other one around the steering wheel and squeezed. Fuck, he couldn't do this, didn't want to drag the past back up, didn't want to remember.

He had to. Sammie deserved to know the truth.

"You don't know what we did over there."

She hesitated, blew out a heavy sigh. "Not details but enough—"

"You. Don't. Know." The words were flat, final. He didn't look at her, he couldn't, so he stared out the window. "We'd go on patrols, day in and day out. Different villages. Never knowing what we'd find."

"Jon—"

He silenced her with a single shake of his head. He didn't want her to interrupt; if she did, he'd never be able to get it out. He had never talked about this with anyone before, nobody except Mac and Daryl. That was different—they were there, they had experienced it. Jonathan had to tell her. Had to let her know—

He took another deep breath and kept staring out the windshield of the car. But he wasn't seeing the parking lot, wasn't seeing the rows of cars or the people walking and laughing.

Hot. The sun beating down, searing his eyes in spite of the dark sunglasses he always wore. The grit of sand in his boots, stuck to his pants and shirt, plastered against the sweaty flesh of his chest and stuck between his fucking teeth.

Ramshackle huts, their color only slightly darker than all that Godforsaken sand, the sea of beige broken by the faded and muted colors of worn blankets or sheets hanging in doorways and windows.

Whispers. Laughter. Suspicious looks from dark eyes, at odds with the forced smiles and calls of welcome.

"We were on one patrol, in some shitty fucking village, checking out some intel. We didn't think there was anything to it. Fuck, there was nothing but women and kids in the village. There couldn't be anything to it."

A shout of warning. A scream. Gunfire and the sound of bullets tearing into flesh.

Blood, dark and red, saturating the sand beneath his feet.

An outstretched hand, the palms scratched and caked with dirt. Lifeless fingers reaching across the desert floor, stretching toward the switch that would kill them all.

Dark eyes, opened to the searing sun beating above them,

the sightless eyes focused on something nobody else could see.

The face, young and unlined, the skin oddly perfect, marred only by the blood seeping from the boy's mouth.

A boy. A fucking kid. No more than ten or eleven. Lifeless.

Because of Jonathan.

Fuck. He could still hear the scream. Still smell the metallic odor of spilled blood, even after all this time.

He closed his eyes, dug the nails of his fingers into the flesh of his palm, reminding himself that he wasn't there anymore.

"The kid was just ten-years-old. Maybe eleven. Just a fucking kid with a fucking bomb strapped to his fucking chest."

He heard Sammie's swift intake of breath, sensed her stiffen in the seat beside him. If he looked over, would he see her condemnation? Would her dark brown eyes be filled with disgust at what he'd just confessed?

Tell her the rest. She deserves to know all of it.

He sucked a ragged breath through his raw throat, squeezed his eyes shut against the scratchy burning sensation. "He was the first kid I killed, Sammie. But he wasn't the last. Kids. Women. Fucking sent out to fucking blow themselves up and take as many of us with them as they could."

Startled silence filled the car, heavy with judgment. Sammie's? His? It didn't matter.

He opened his eyes and stared straight ahead, afraid to move his head to the side even the tiniest bit. Afraid he'd see revulsion reflected in Sammie's beautiful brown eyes. He couldn't bear to see that, not now.

Not ever.

"I turned into a monster over there. And I couldn't come back to you like that. How could I, after what I'd done, after what I'd become? How could I even think of touching you after that? And to hold Clare, to taint her innocence with the blood on my hands? I couldn't. You deserved better. Both of you. So I did what I thought was best. I set you free."

And fuck, could she even hear him, with the way his voice shook and cracked? With the way the whispered words were ripped from his aching chest? He didn't know, wasn't sure if he even wanted to know. He wasn't sure of anything, not now, not after telling her.

"Jon." His name was nothing more than a ragged whisper falling from her lips. He closed his eyes and shook his head, unwilling to hear her voice her loathing. Her fear. Her condemnation.

"You—you should just go now." And fuck, it hurt to tell her that, hurt to set her free. This wasn't what he wanted, wasn't what he had hoped for. But he'd been a fool to think telling her would change anything. The only thing telling her had done was convince him once more that she deserved so much better.

Long minutes dragged by, the quiet passing of time so oppressive it hurt to breathe. Then he heard the passenger door open, felt a rush of cold night air wash over him as Sammie climbed out of the car.

The door slammed behind her, hard and loud. The noise startled him and he opened his eyes, forced himself to watch as she hurried across the parking lot, moving further away from him with each brisk step.

Sammie had wanted closure. Had ripping the soul from his chest provided it for her? It didn't matter because he'd do it again. He'd do anything for her.

Because she *was* his soul.

chapter
TWELVE

Flames licked at the logs, the oranges and reds casting a glow as gentle and hypnotizing as the heat drifting from the fireplace. Sammie usually found the sight to be soothing. Relaxing. Tonight should be no different.

Family was gathered in the large Victorian farmhouse, children chattering and laughing, adults talking in low tones, plans being made for the annual tree-cutting expedition and good-natured arguments over which child would be responsible for putting the angel on top once the tree was decorated. Sammie was surrounded by family: her parents; her two sisters and their husbands and kids; her mother's brother and his wife. Dinner was finished, leftovers had been put away, and coffee was brewing for dessert.

Families. Whole and unbroken and happy.

Everyone except her own.

In spite of the noise and togetherness that

permeated the house, Sammie felt alone. Isolated. Her mind wasn't on dessert or the annual trek to get the tree, or even the get-together the team was planning for Sunday.

Her mind was on Jon, on everything he had told her last night. She couldn't get the words out of her head, couldn't get the images from her mind. His words hadn't been graphic, and she knew instinctively that he'd deliberately left out details. But what he'd told her was enough—more than enough. It was too easy to imagine what he'd seen and done. Too easy to imagine what he must have felt—what he still felt.

Sammie closed her eyes and tried to banish the images that had plagued her ever since he told her. The images had even haunted her in her sleep—what little sleep she'd had last night.

Worse than the images was the guilt she felt. What had it cost Jon to open up to her like that? She didn't know. And instead of staying around long enough to find out, she had climbed out of his car when he told her to leave and hurried to her own, needing to put space between them, needing to run from the horrifying images flashing in her mind.

And if merely *hearing* those things had upset her, what had actually experiencing them done to Jon?

No, she owed him nothing. They were no longer married, and he was no longer part of her life—hadn't been for more than two years.

Except that was a lie. Jon would always be part of her life—

Because of Clare.

She glanced over, a small smile spreading across her face as she watched her daughter help her cousins build something out of blocks. Clare's assistance generally involved knocking the blocks over after they reached a certain height, then giggling as her cousins set them up again.

Did she see any of Jon in their daughter? Clare had Sammie's curly hair and wide brown eyes. The shape of her mouth was almost identical to Sammie's mother's. Everyone always commented how much Clare resembled Sammie that she never looked for anything of Jon in her.

Watching her daughter now, she wondered if she had deliberately ignored the small resemblances, or if she had simply been blind to them. Because there *were* resemblances: the structure of Clare's cheekbones, finally emerging as she got older; the set of her eyes, so similar to Jon's; the shape of her nose, showing more than a hint of her father.

The father Clare had never seen, not since she was only a few months old.

The father who was afraid to see her because he was convinced he was a monster. Afraid that seeing her or holding her would somehow taint her.

Sammie blinked back the tears burning her eyes and turned her gaze to the fire. Jon had missed his daughter's first tooth, first word. He had missed Clare learning to crawl and walk. He had no idea what it felt like to hold his daughter's warm body against him as he read her a bedtime story, to hear her gentle breathing as she fell asleep or to kiss her soft cheek as he tucked her in.

Because he was convinced he was a monster.

Sammie couldn't wrap her head around it. How could he think that? What he'd done—those were things he'd had to do to survive. Would he have rather died over there? Couldn't he see that he hadn't had a choice?

Maybe he did. Sammie didn't know. He had never bothered to talk to her about it, had never bothered to give them a chance to work through it.

Had never bothered giving her the chance to support him.

Had never given her a choice.

Did that mean he should never be part of Clare's life?

No.

But shouldn't he be the one to make the first move?

As much as Sammie would like to say yes, she knew he never would, not after everything he'd told her. She didn't want to understand his reasoning, didn't want to sympathize, but she did.

No matter what may have happened between them, no matter how much he had hurt her by walking away the way he had, he didn't deserve to be estranged from his own daughter.

Sammie sighed and leaned her head against the sofa, her gaze drifting over to her own father. Big, loud, larger than life. Always there for his family. A rock, even in times of upheaval—like her and her sisters' teenage years. Sammie tried to imagine what life would have been like growing up without her father. No matter how hard she tried, she couldn't. Her father had been too large an influence on her life. He still was.

Didn't Clare deserve the same thing?

But what if Sammie did this, and Jon walked away again? He'd done it once, nothing was stopping him from doing it again.

But what if he *didn't* do it again? Was it right for her to take that chance away from him and his daughter?

Sammie wished she could talk to someone about this, wished there was someone she could discuss her fears and hopes with, someone who would listen and play devil's advocate and give her advice. But there wasn't anyone.

She glanced over at the family gathered in the large dining room, laughing and talking. She couldn't ask her sisters or their husbands, they would never understand. And certainly not her parents. Sammie had never told them all the details, but that wouldn't make a difference—they were firmly anti-Jon at the moment, had been since she moved back here, freshly divorced with a six-month-old infant and no place to call home.

And she couldn't talk to any of her teammates, not about this. Taylor was convinced she should just move on. Shannon thought she needed closure before moving on. And the others...well, none of them really knew the details, and Sammie had no plans to tell them.

Which meant the decision was hers, and hers alone.

"Hey, Boo. Come here with Mommy."

Clare looked up from the block tower she had been ready to knock over then frowned. And oh God, that was Jon's frown, no doubt about it. Sammie swallowed against the sudden lump in her throat then forced a smile to her face.

"Don't even think about saying no, young lady. Come here, Mommy wants to ask you something."

The frown disappeared from Clare's face and she hurried over to Sammie, jumping in her lap with a quiet giggle and wrapping her small arms around Sammie's neck. "What, Mommy?"

"You feel like going for a ride with Mommy?"

Clare laughed then jumped up and down, making Sammie wince when one of her feet connected with her kneecap. "Yes. Yes, yes, yes."

"Go get your shoes and some toys while I get ready." Sammie dropped a kiss on the top of Clare's head before she scampered off then pushed herself up from the floor. Both of her parents watched her as she moved toward the kitchen, their gazes curious and questioning.

"You didn't tell us you had plans, dear."

"Um, yeah. I didn't before." Sammie tossed a smile at her mom then grabbed a large, flat container from one of the cabinets and started going through the leftovers. Turkey. Stuffing. Mashed potatoes and gravy. Sauerkraut and kielbasa. Two rolls. No, make that three.

Her father moved into the kitchen and leaned against the counter, his arms crossed in front of him. His dark eyes followed her as she grabbed another container, smaller this time.

"Sam, what exactly are you doing?"

"Just, um, putting some food together, that's all." She spooned out some cranberry sauce, added a few slices of cold ham and a couple deviled eggs, tossed in some of the raw veggies from the platter in the refrigerator.

"Who's the food for?"

"Um—" Sammie focused on snapping the lids on both containers, trying to figure out how to answer. She didn't want to lie to her parents, but she didn't feel like getting a lecture, either.

"Samantha. What, exactly, are you doing?"

She winced at her father's use of her full name then turned to face him, hoping there wouldn't be a battle over this. "I'm taking Clare to see her father. I thought I'd take some food with me."

Silence greeted her words. Not just silence from her parents, but from her sisters and their husbands, as well. Her mother pushed away from the table and hurried toward them, placing a steadying hand on her father's arm. One glance at their faces told Sammie all she needed to know.

"No. Absolutely not."

Her mother squeezed her father's arm, either reassuring him or trying to silence him, then turned back to Sammie. "I don't think that's a good idea, dear."

"Probably not," Sammie agreed. She placed both containers into a large carry-tote and zipped it up. "But I'm doing it anyway."

"I don't—"

"Dad, please. It's something I need to do, okay?"

"Are you thinking about getting back with him?"

"No." Sammie shook her head. Of that, she was positive. This wasn't about her. This wasn't about a reconciliation. This was about Clare, nothing else. She told them that, her voice as clear and adamant as she could make it. But she saw the doubt in their eyes and readied herself for more objections, wondering if this was going to lead to a huge family squabble.

Clare came running in, dragging her small backpack behind her and holding one tiny shoe up. "Ready, Mommy!"

Sammie laughed, grateful for the distraction. She scooped Clare up and sat her on the counter, then busied herself with untying the knot in the shoe and getting it on her daughter's foot.

"You're making a mistake—"

"Dad, I know—"

"I forbid you to leave this house."

Sam blinked, her mouth hanging open in surprise. She snapped it closed, darted a glance toward her mother, then looked back at her father. "Dad, I'm twenty-four. You can't *forbid* me to do anything."

"As long as you live in my house—"

"Dennis. Stop." Her mother's calm voice eased some of the tension that had spiked at her father's words. "Sammie, you need to think about what you're doing. Think about the possible repercussions—"

"I have, Mom. This is something I need to do. Okay?" She held her mother's gaze for several long minutes, silently willing her to understand. Did she? Sammie wasn't sure. How could she expect her mother to understand, when she wasn't sure she understood herself? But her mother slowly nodded, although the worry was still clear in her eyes.

Sammie heaved a sigh of relief then lowered Clare to the floor and grabbed the tote filled with leftovers. "I won't be too late."

She ushered Clare to the door, bundled her in her coat and hat and mittens, then shrugged into her own coat and gloves before moving outside.

It wasn't until she reached the end of the long driveway that she realized she had no idea where Jon lived.

chapter **THIRTEEN**

"You, my man, are a complete fucking idiot."

Jonathan paused with the bottle halfway to his mouth, just long enough to shoot Mac a death glare, then took a long swallow. The beer was just this side of lukewarm and too bitter. His lips twisted in a grimace and he placed the bottle back on the low table in front of him.

Mac ignored the glare and kept talking, calling him every name in the book and some he just decided to make up. Jonathan tuned him out, trying to focus on the football game playing out on the television across the room.

Then Daryl started in, adding his own colorful insults and ruining any chance Jonathan had of focusing on the game.

"Seriously. What the hell were you thinking?"

"I was thinking she had a right to know."

"Not about that. *That*, I get. But you don't just

fucking drop shit like that on someone with no experience. No wonder she ran off. You probably scared the fuck out of her."

"She didn't *run off*." Not really. Jonathan had simply told her to leave—and she did.

Mac laughed, the sound a gravelly bark of sharp noise. "Yeah. Uh-huh. Knowing you, you probably told her to leave."

"What the fuck were you even thinking?" Daryl repeated the question around a mouthful of cold pizza. "You totally ruined our plan of making the former Mrs. Reigler the future Mrs. Reigler."

"There was no plan."

"The hell there wasn't." Daryl tossed the crust into the opened pizza box then grabbed a napkin and swiped it across his mouth. "You were supposed to ease into it. Get her used to seeing you again. Let her get comfortable with you. Let her get to know you again. Not strongarm her into meeting you in some stupid fucking parking lot then dropping that fucking bombshell on her. Hell, I would have run off, too."

"Yeah, well. Not like it matters. None of this shit was going to work anyway."

"Fuck. Not with that attitude, it wasn't." Mac leaned back on the sofa, draping both arms along the back, then turned to study Jonathan. Intense. Serious. Seeing way too much.

Jonathan shifted and looked away, wishing again that he hadn't said anything to either of his buddies. Telling them had been a mistake.

But who the hell else was he going to talk to? The three of them had been through hell together—more than once. They had each other's backs, no matter what. They were more than buddies. More than comrades. They were brothers—closer than brothers.

"Okay, so Plan A didn't work. Now we just need to come up with Plan B. And make sure you stick to it this time."

"No, no Plan B. Or C or D or anything else. It's done. Time to move on to something else." And fuck, why did saying that hurt so much? Jonathan had known, even before moving back here, that this wasn't going to work. Sammie was no longer part of his life. She had moved on—and he had helped her do just that by giving her the closure she needed.

Yeah. That was really fucking big of him.

Fuck.

He swallowed back the bitterness threatening to overwhelm him and changed the subject. "So when does the contract get finalized?"

"Trying to change the subject, huh?"

"There is no subject. That subject is over. Done. Closed."

"You're a fucking fool."

"Thanks for your support."

"I just don't understand—"

"Yeah, you do." Jonathan met Daryl's unflinching gaze, refusing to look away. Refusing to hide his deepest thoughts. Daryl heaved a sigh then sat back and placed the heels of his boots on the coffee table.

"I head back to DC Monday. Everything should be finalized by then."

Mac leaned forward and grabbed the last slice of pizza. "And then what?"

"Then we finalize the financing we need and start from there. Should be a piece of cake."

"That's still a hell of a lot of money. And lining up the equipment—"

"It's already lined up. I told you that."

"Well, I'll feel a lot better when the shit's in our possession."

Mac snorted his agreement. "Yeah. And when we actually get our first big fucking job. I'm getting antsy, doing all this little shit. Nothing more than busy work. I need some action."

"We're doing okay so far. We all knew this was going to be slow-going. And we have that gig with the Blades now, remember?"

"Um, about that—" Jonathan cleared his throat, exchanged a quiet look with Mac, then turned to Daryl. "It's a shit job, and you know it. We need to let it go. Farm it out. Something. That's not what we do, and you know it."

"Yeah, I know. I was just trying to help you out."

"Well, you can unhelp. We need to unload it."

"No, I don't think so."

Jonathan and Mac both opened their mouths to voice their disagreement, but Daryl cut them off with a brush of his hand. "We're not unloading it. It's a nice little side gig that isn't costing us anything."

"You mean other than time and money?"

"I already have that taken care of. I lined up a couple of guys to take over. What we're getting more than makes up for their pay."

"Why would you even waste time—"

"Because of the contacts. The team's owner is a big name in the private sector. You know as well as I do that connections are everything in this business. Add that to the contract we're getting from DC, and we'll be set."

"You really think this is going to work?"

"Yeah, I do. Trust me—in six months, we're going

to have more work than we can handle. Which means we need to start adding some talent, get names lined up."

Jonathan settled back on the sofa, letting Daryl's words sink in. Six months ago, the three of them had said goodbye to the military and moved here to start their own personal security firm. It had been nothing more than a half-baked idea back then, something to talk about to take their minds off the hell they lived every day. But at some point, the aimless chatter had turned into a real plan, one that grew a little clearer with each passing day, until Cover Six Security became a reality.

They'd been doing odd jobs, nothing big or newsworthy unless you counted the payout, while Daryl worked his contacts to open the door to the gray networks that worked behind the scenes of the polished surface of DC politics. Their patience was finally paying off.

Which suited Jonathan just fine, especially now. He needed something to get his mind off everything else. Had he really thought he could make Sammie forget what he'd done?

Yeah, he had, in that small fantasy that lived deep inside him.

Which was fucking stupid. So fucking stupid. He should have known better. Maybe, deep down, he *had*. Yeah, right. Sure he had. That's why the disappointment still ate at him, slowly chewing away what was left of his fucking soul.

"Snap out of, Reigler."

Jonathan looked over, surprised at the sharpness of Mac's voice. "I'm fine."

"Bullshit. You're moping."

"I said I'm fine."

"You're a fucking liar."

"And I said—"

"Would you two knock it the fuck off? You're like two little kids, and you're giving me a headache." Daryl's quiet voice broke into their bickering, silencing them. Jonathan tossed a last dirty look at Mach then pushed up from the sofa.

"I'm grabbing another beer. Anyone want anything?"

"Yeah, I'll take one."

"Might as well make it three."

Jonathan grunted, grabbed the empty pizza box and bottles from the coffee table, then made his way into the kitchen. He heard the low hum of conversation, Daryl and Mac discussing strategy and plans, but he didn't pay attention. He was too focused on Mac's accusations.

Was he moping? Yeah.

Was he a liar? About this, probably. He had hoped, prayed, that he'd get that second chance. But the guys were right—he had fucked up. Again.

It didn't matter. Sammie had deserved to know. And if telling her had given her the closure she needed...well, he could only hope for her happiness.

Yeah, because he was fucking honorable like that. Yes, he wanted Sammie to be happy. But dammit, he had really thought she could find that happiness with him.

Fuck.

The sound of the doorbell chiming startled him. He wasn't expecting company, had no idea who it could be. And he wasn't in the mood to deal with anyone. Hell, just dealing with Mac and Daryl was enough of a challenge today.

He dumped the pizza crusts into the trashcan then popped his head around the corner. "Can one of you get that? And get rid of whoever it is."

"Yeah. Sure. Whatever." Mac kept grumbling as he got to his feet. Jonathan simply ignored him and went back to cleaning up, bending the pizza box in half so he could jam it into the trash can.

He heard the door open, heard the odd silence that followed. And then he heard a voice that made him wonder if he was hallucinating, made him wonder if he had finally lost it.

"I'm sorry. I was looking for Jon Reigler."

Chapter FOURTEEN

Sammie stood just outside the door, her purse, Clare's backpack, and the tote bag filled with leftovers in one hand. Her other hand was wrapped around Clare's, trying to hold her still. Her daughter kept squirming, clinging to her leg then moving to her side so she could peek up at the man who answered the door. He was tall, broad, with a military haircut and a gruesome scar that sliced across the lower half of his face. Sammie forced herself not to stare, forced herself not to turn and run.

"I'm sorry. I was looking for Jon Reigler." Had she said that already? She thought maybe she had because the man smiled down at her and stepped back. The smile transformed his face, but Sammie wasn't sure if that was a good thing or not. And she certainly wasn't about to step inside, even if he was inviting her in.

The man's brows shot up in something that might have been amusement. Or maybe it was just a silent acknowledgment of her stares, like he knew she was unable to stop being so rude.

She forced her gaze from his face and glanced down at Clare, expecting to see her daughter trying to hide from the strange man and the gruesome scars covering his face. But Clare wasn't trying to hide, and she didn't look scared at all. She looked fascinated. Curious, even, with her head tilted to the side as she studied him.

"You've come to the right place. He's in the kitchen." The man looked over his shoulder and raised his voice. "Hey, Reigler. Your wife and daughter are here."

The words shocked Sammie. How did he know who she was? Heat rushed to her face and she shook her head. "I'm not his wife—"

"Ex-wife then. For now." The man smiled again then dropped to one knee, wiggling his large fingers at Clare in a silly wave that looked totally at odds with the man himself. "And aren't you completely adorable? You don't look a thing like your dad. That's probably a good thing. I'm Mac. What's your name?"

Sammie tugged on Clare's hand, ready to pull her down the hallway and out the door. But her daughter stepped out from behind her legs and offered the man a wide smile.

"I Clare."

"'I *am* Clare.'" Sammie automatically corrected her then winced. What was she doing? She shouldn't be standing here, correcting her daughter's grammar. She should be running out to the car, fleeing to safety. She had called Jon's sister, asking for his address even though she hadn't seen or talked to Crissy in over a year. Had the woman sent Sammie to the wrong place on purpose? Was this supposed to be some kind of joke?

No, it couldn't be, not when the man kneeling in front of Clare seemed to know who they were.

"Nice to meet you, Clare." The man glanced up at Sammie, the smile on his face growing a little wider, as if trying to reassure her. Clare stepped forward and patted the man's mouth with one tiny hand.

"Boo-boo."

"Clare!" Sammie reached for her, ready to apologize, but the man simply laughed.

"Yes, it certainly is."

"Christ, Mac. Let them in before you give the kid nightmares."

The voice startled Sammie and she looked around, surprised to see a second man approaching the door. He was a few inches shorter, not quite as large as the first man, with a warm smile that should have put her at ease.

It didn't.

"I'm Daryl. And you must be Sammie. We've heard a lot about you."

"I—" Sammie closed her mouth and tried to swallow back the apprehension threatening to overwhelm her. This had been a bad idea, such a bad idea. "I'm sorry. I wasn't thinking—we should probably—"

"Come in and make yourself comfortable. Here, let me take that." Daryl took the large tote bag from her hand, somehow easing her into the small apartment at the same time. The door closed behind her and she jumped, her hand automatically reaching for Clare's as she tugged her daughter behind her.

"Jon's in the kitchen. Probably hyperventilating or

something. I'll take this into him." Daryl unzipped the tote and looked inside. "Or maybe I'll just eat it myself. Smells wonderful."

"I really should go—"

"Nonsense. Jon should be out in a minute. Have a seat, make yourself comfortable." Daryl offered her what she supposed was meant to be a reassuring smile then disappeared down a short hallway. She didn't move, not even when the other man—Mac—stepped around her and took a seat on the leather sofa a few feet away.

"I read that article about you last week. I don't know much about hockey but I was impressed. Sounds like a lot of hard work."

"Oh. Um, thank you." Oh God, what was she doing, thanking this complete stranger? She needed to scoop Clare up and make a mad dash for the door.

A dull thud echoed from what she assumed was the kitchen, followed by a low rush of words she couldn't make out. Her gaze darted down the hall then snapped back to the man lounging on the sofa. He grinned, acting like he hadn't heard the noise at all.

"The article said you were a teacher, too. Kindergarten, right?"

"Yes."

Another thud echoed from the kitchen, a little louder this time. There were more words, still low and rushed, but she thought she could make out something that sounded suspiciously like the f-bomb, followed by the words *head* and *ass*.

She bent down and lifted Clare into her arms then slowly backed toward the door. "This is a bad time. We'll just leave—"

"Daryl's just having a little chit-chat with Jon. I'm

sure he'll be out in a minute. Are you sure you don't want to have a seat? Get comfortable while you wait?"

Sammie shook her head and backed up another step, ready to bolt. Daryl stepped out of the kitchen, a smile on his face and what looked like a red mark on his jaw. He nodded at Sammie then looked over at Mac.

"We're leaving."

"And miss this? Are you crazy?"

"Now, MacGregor. That's an order."

Mac rolled his eyes but stood and headed toward the door. He stopped in front of Clare and lifted his hand, holding it palm-out toward her daughter. Clare didn't hesitate at all, just leaned forward and slapped the other man's hand in an enthusiastic high-five.

"See you around, Munchkin. Don't give your dad too much grief."

"Mac. Now." Daryl pulled two coats from the rack near the door and tossed one at Mac. He shrugged into his own then nodded toward Sammie. "Ma'am, nice meeting you. Jon will be out in a few minutes. He's, uh, he's cleaning something up."

And then they were both gone, leaving Sammie standing there in the middle of the room, holding Clare in her arms as she wondered what was going on. How long did she stay like that? Seconds? Minutes? Long enough that her arm started to ache from Clare's weight. Long enough that Clare started getting restless and pushed against her, trying to get down.

She rubbed a hand over her daughter's back, trying to settle her down. "No, Boo. Not yet."

There was still no sign of Jon, nothing more than an occasional sound or two coming from the kitchen, sounds she couldn't decipher.

Sammie looked around, her eyes barely registering the neat yet spartan layout of the apartment as she wondered what she should do. Leave? Go look for Jon?

Leave. Yes, she should leave. But she couldn't quite make her feet work, not when those sounds coming from the kitchen filled her with—

With what? Apprehension? Fear?

No, neither of those. Maybe she was being foolish, maybe the smartest thing she could do was turn and run, but there was something about those sounds—

She lowered Clare to her feet then bent down in front of her and pushed the backpack into her daughter's hands. "You stay here, Boo. Okay? Mommy needs to check on something."

"'Kay." Clare nodded, already busying herself with opening the backpack and digging through it. Sammie pressed a kiss to the top of her head then stood, each step hesitant as she moved down the hall toward the kitchen.

Then froze when she reached the doorway.

Jon was leaning against the counter, his back to her. The knuckles of both hands were stark white as he gripped the countertop. His head was lowered, his broad shoulders hunched and stiff. His entire body was rigid, as if he had been turned to stone.

No, that wasn't right. His shoulders moved as she watched, heaved up and down as he sucked in deep, ragged breaths. Sammie's heart slammed into her chest and her stomach clenched. She took a step toward him, stopped. Another step then stopped again.

"Jon?"

"Yeah." His voice was hoarse, the word barely more than a croak. His shoulders moved again, his hands tightening even more around the edge of the countertop. "Just, uh. Just give me a minute."

"Jon, is everything—" She closed her mouth before she could finish the sentence. She had been ready to ask him if everything was okay, and how stupid was that when it was so obvious that it wasn't?

She hesitated, almost turned and walked out of the kitchen. But there was something about the way he was standing, something about the way he gripped the countertop, like a drowning man desperately clinging to a piece of burning wreckage, that stopped her. She closed the distance between them, reached out and placed her hand on his forearm.

It was like touching a statue. His skin was cold to the touch, the muscles pulled tight, tense, hard as a rock. He shuddered at her touch, slowly turned his head and looked down at her.

Sammie's hand tightened on his arm as the breath left her in a rush. His eyes were unnaturally bright, catching the reflection of the overhead light. A muscle jumped in his clenched jaw and his sculpted mouth was pulled tight, the flesh of his lips so pale, they were almost white. And the look on his face, in his eyes as they searched hers—she had never seen such a look of desperation, of pain and agony. The emotions rolling off his tense body slammed into her, and she had to blink back her own tears as something inside her cracked.

She hadn't stopped to think what seeing Clare might do to him. She hadn't stopped to think at all, afraid she'd lose her nerve and turn back around. But Jon hadn't seen his daughter in almost three years. She couldn't imagine what he must be feeling.

She didn't have to imagine, not when she could

see it—*feel* it—so clearly, like a knife slicing through her heart.

She watched as his strong throat worked, as he forced hoarse words from his pale, trembling lips.

"Sammie, I don't think I can do this."

She tightened her hand on his arm and reached out with her other one, gently rubbing circles against his back—much like she did when trying to soothe Clare. But Jon's back was broader, harder, the muscles bunching under her touch. The heat of his skin beneath the thin t-shirt scorched her palm.

"Yes. You can." She leaned closer, her lips trembling as she offered him a small smile. "You're not a monster, Jon."

Something flashed in his eyes. Surprise? Hope? Disbelief? Sammie couldn't tell, thought maybe it was a combination of all three. She opened her mouth, ready to offer him more reassurances, when Clare came running into the kitchen, a book held in one hand and her favorite stuffed bear in the other.

The same bear Jon had given her right after she was born, when it was almost as big as she had been.

She heard Jon's swift intake of breath, felt his body stiffen even more as he turned around and stared down at his daughter. Then he made a noise, an odd kind of strangling sound, and slid to the floor.

Sammie gasped and dropped to her knees, wondering if Jon had fainted. No, of course he hadn't. He shook his head, offered her a faint wave of one hand, and pulled in a deep breath.

"I'm fine."

He didn't sound fine, but Sammie didn't bother telling him that. She settled on the floor next to him, crossed her legs at the ankle, then tapped a hand against her thigh.

"Come here, Boo. I want you to meet someone."

Clare didn't hesitate, just took a running leap and jumped into her lap. Sammie bit back a groan, heard something that might have been choked laughter coming from Jon. She settled Clare on her lap then reached up to unzip her coat. "She's heavier than she looks. I think I have more bruises on my legs from her than I do from hockey."

Jon just sat there, his gaze focused on his daughter as Sammie tugged Clare's arms from the coat sleeves. She had to juggle first the bear then the book to do it, because Clare didn't want to let go of either. She kept up a running commentary, mindless words about things Clare liked to do, wondering if Jon was even listening.

Yes, he was. He heard every single word, seemed to be committing them to memory as he watched his daughter. Sammie folded the coat and placed it on the floor next to her, then wrapped one arm around Clare and ruffled her hair with the other.

"Clare, this is—" Sammie stopped, her throat closing up as she struggled with the next words. How should she introduce Jon? She couldn't tell Clare he was her father, not yet. Or could she? No, not yet. She didn't want to confuse her, didn't want to complicate things. But she hadn't thought things through, hadn't even considered what to tell Clare.

Jon must have sensed her hesitation because he leaned forward and gave Clare a small smile. "Jon. I'm Jon."

Clare repeated his name then giggled. But instead of snuggling up to Sammie like she'd been expecting, Clare climbed off her lap and straight into Jon's, clutching the bear to her chest as she held the book out to him, almost knocking him in the chin with it.

The smile disappeared from Jon's rugged face, replaced with a look of panic and fear. Sammie placed a hand on his arm, gave it a reassuring squeeze. "It's okay, Jon. She won't break."

"But I—" His mouth snapped shut and his throat worked as he swallowed. The panic and uncertainty slowly left his eyes as Clare curled up in his lap, her back against his chest. She looked at him over her shoulder, her brown eyes so trusting, then held the book up to him.

"Read me story. Now."

A startled laugh fell from Jon's mouth. He looked over at Sammie, one brow raised in surprise. "She's a bossy one, huh?"

"Not bossy. Determined."

"Yeah, okay." He settled back against the cabinets and reached for the book, flipping through the colorful pages before turning back to the first one. He paused, his gaze steady on hers, filled with unspoken questions.

Dread filled Sammie and she quickly moved away from Jon, surprised to realize that her leg had been pressed against his. She shook her head. "This isn't about us, Jon. That hasn't changed. And it won't. But that doesn't mean you can't be in Clare's life."

He didn't say anything for the longest time, just sat there, watching her, his dark gaze entirely too focused and penetrating. She could see the unspoken words, could *hear* them in her head as he watched her.

Not yet.

She shook her head again, ready to tell him that this changed nothing, when Clare turned around and placed one hand against her father's cheek, turning his head so he was looking at the book.

"Read me story. *Now*."

Sammie's stomach clenched when she heard the tone of her daughter's voice. What had Jon said? That Clare was bossy?

And she had assured him she wasn't bossy, just determined.

It was only now that she realized where Clare had inherited that trait—

From her father.

chapter FIFTEEN

"Okay, Reigs, spill it. Why is your husband here?"
"Yeah. I thought you told him to get lost."
Sammie slid to a stop by the boards, Shannon and Taylor right beside her. They both stared at her, their faces filled with concern—and curiosity.

Sammie sighed, her gaze drifting from her teammates down to the other end of the ice. Jon was bent over, Clare's small mitten-covered hands in his as they shuffled and drifted across the ice, an inch at a time. The sight caused her heart to squeeze, but she didn't know if it was from seeing Clare with her father—or from the expression of amazement and wonder on Jon's face.

She hadn't meant to invite him today, had never even stopped to consider it. Today was a post-Thanksgiving team get-together, a family day of sorts to bring the team and their friends and family together for some time on the ice with pizza afterward. The idea had been Taylor's, who said something to Chuckie, who said something to Mr. Murphy, who thought it would be a great idea and promptly made plans for the Blades to have the ice to themselves. And Chuckie, in his never-ending quest for PR, had decided to invite some press.

If Sammie had known that, she would have never invited Jon—not that she had planned on inviting him, period. The words had just slipped out before her brain had engaged, the other night as she was leaving his apartment.

Sammie sighed again, the breath leaving her in a small cloud of vapor that quickly disappeared in the chilled air. Shannon and Taylor were still watching her, silently demanding an answer.

"It was an accident."

Shannon's brows shot up in surprise. "An accident? How do you *accidentally* invite your ex-husband to a team get-together?"

"I don't know. It just—I opened my mouth to say goodnight and the next thing I know, I'm telling him about today and asking if he wants to come. It wasn't on purpose." Sammie shifted her weight from one skate to the other, not quite able to meet her teammates' questioning gazes. "I mean, if you could have seen him with Clare, seen his face and the way he acted and how...how *good* he was with her—"

"Wait. Hang on. Back the fuck up. When did this happen? Because when we talked last week, you sounded pretty adamant that you wanted to get rid of him."

"I know."

"So then what the hell happened?"

Sammie met Shannon's gaze then quickly looked

away. She chewed on her lower lip, trying to decide what to tell them, then shook her head. Nodded. Shook her head again.

"You look like a puppet."

"What?"

"You heard me." Taylor leaned forward and placed her hand on the top of Sammie's head. "All that head-bobbing makes you look like a puppet. Out with it already."

"I don't think—"

"Tit-for-tat. You tell us your secret. And I'll tell you mine."

"You're pregnant."

"What!" Taylor's screech echoed across the ice. She cringed then elbowed Shannon in the side, hard enough to make the other woman stumble. "God, no. Just—wow. Not just no, but hell no. How does your mind even work? I mean, seriously."

"Oh, come on. We all know you and Chuckie got this big thing going on. Don't tell me you're not doing your hottie every chance you get."

"There is something seriously wrong with your brain. You know that, right? I mean, for real. It's wired wrong or something."

"Hey, I'm a goalie. We're known for being weird."

Sammie started backing away, just a little at a time, hoping to use their friendly bickering to make her escape. Taylor and Shannon each grabbed one of her arms and pulled her back, not even looking at her.

"Whatever. I'm not pregnant so don't even go there. And you—" Taylor finally faced Sammie. "Out with it. What happened?"

"Yeah, Reigs. Details. Now."

"It—well...I—" Sammie cleared her throat and

aimed her gaze at a scuff mark running along the boards. "I talked to him Wednesday night, just for closure, you know. Like you said. And he—"

No, she wouldn't tell them everything Jon had said, about what had happened and the things he'd seen and done. That was between the two of them. Even if it wasn't, she'd never tell them.

She cleared her throat again and shrugged. "I don't know. I guess—I guess I understand why he did what he did a little better now. And then I was home on Thanksgiving, watching Clare play with her cousins, and thinking about all the things Jon had missed and all the things I used to do with *my* dad when I was growing up and how Clare was missing out on those things so…so I took her over to see him. And then, when I was leaving, it just kind of slipped out about today and before I knew it, I had invited him along."

Silence greeted the rush of words. Sammie chewed on her lower lip for a few seconds then finally raised her gaze. Shannon and Taylor were both watching her, with oddly blank expressions on their faces. A few more seconds crawled by before Shannon leaned closer, a wide smile on her face.

"So. You sleeping with him?"

"No! God, no. Holy crappola, Shannon. Just, no. Taylor's right, there's something seriously wrong with your brain."

"What? I mean, it's a perfectly normal question. You guys were married. He's Clare's father. And he's a serious hottie, with those rugged good looks and all that dark intensity. Don't tell me you haven't thought about it."

"No. I haven't." But Sammie couldn't meet Shannon's eyes, and she couldn't hide the blush that scorched her cheeks.

"I think you're lying."

Taylor spun on her skates, a frown creasing her forehead as she stared at the opposite end of the ice. "Well, if you ask me, she'd be a fool to sleep with him. After what he did to her? No way."

Sammie opened her mouth to defend Jon then quickly snapped it shut. Why was she going to defend him? Taylor was right—and she was only repeating what Sammie had said at least a hundred times, whenever Taylor had asked her about her ex.

"Say what you want, LeBlanc, but you're wrong. I've got twenty bucks that says they're doing the wild thing by Christmas."

"Deal."

"Guys, I'm standing right here. You know that, right?"

"Yeah. So?"

Sammie rolled her eyes, not sure if she should laugh or scream or cry. It didn't matter because in the end, *she'd* have the last laugh. Let them both bet—she wasn't going to sleep with Jon. Ever. It was over between them, had been for more than two years.

"It's probably a good thing you don't want him, anyway. Rachel-the-bitch is already moving in."

"What?" Sammie moved her gaze past Shannon, down to where Jon was still puttering on the ice with Clare. Sure enough, Rachel Woodhouse was standing there with them, an inviting smile on her face. She placed her hand on Jon's arm, the gesture somehow possessive, and leaned in closer, saying something to him.

Anger swept over Sammie—along with an irrational spurt of jealousy. No, it wasn't jealousy. It couldn't be. It was nothing more than her dislike for the woman shooting to the surface, that was all. Sammie was just reading the emotion wrong.

Because there was no way she was jealous. Absolutely no way.

Then why did she want to go over and tear every single strand of platinum blonde hair from Rachel's head, then scratch those stupid blue eyes from her face?

"Down, girl."

"What?" Sammie turned, surprised to see Taylor and Shannon watching her with amusement. Taylor finally rolled her eyes then moved her gaze to Shannon.

"I changed my mind. No bet. You're right—she's going to sleep with him."

"No, I am not." Sammie ground each word from between clenched teeth. She sucked in a deep breath, let it out nice and slow, then forced a smile to her face. "I just don't think it's very professional to come on to a man when her daughter is right. There. With. Him."

"Wow. You're kind of scary-ferocious right now, Reigs. This a whole new side to you. I like it."

"Oh, shut up." Sammie ignored their laughter and started to move past them, ready to—well, she wasn't sure *what* she was going to do. All she knew was that she wanted Rachel *away* from Jon.

No, she mentally corrected, away from *Clare*. She wasn't concerned about Jon.

She didn't go very far because Shannon and Taylor both grabbed her arms again, pulling her back. She tried tugging her arms from their grasp but Taylor simply shook her head, then nodded to where Jon and Clare were standing.

"Wait. Watch."

"I'd rather not—"

"No, seriously. Can't you see?"

No, Sammie couldn't see. She was still too angry. Too—no, she absolutely was *not* jealous. "See what?"

"He's shutting her down."

"That's not a shut-down—that's a total *fuck off*! This is fucking great!"

Sammie blinked then forced herself to focus on the spectacle at the other end of the ice. Sure enough, Jon's entire body had stiffened. Even from this far away, she could see the way his jaw clenched, the way the muscle jumped along the side of his cheek. And he didn't just shrug Rachel's hand from his arm—he actually *brushed it off* and then stepped back from her as he shook his head. Then he turned his back on Rachel and glided away from her, still holding onto Clare.

"Oh man, I wish I had a camera. That was abso-fucking-lutely beautiful. Damn."

Sammie didn't say anything, could barely even grunt in agreement. Her heart was lodged somewhere in her throat, her blood rushing through her veins, dangerously close to the surface of her skin. She felt...warm. Prickly. Unsettled. And she had the sudden urge to rush over to Jon, to place her own hand on his arm in that same possessive manner that Rachel had used.

Like she was *claiming* him.

Holy crappola. No. No, no, no.

Sammie blinked and gave her head a quick shake, dislodging each irrational thought. She was simply overreacting because she didn't like Rachel, that's all there was to it. A simple, rational, easily-explained reaction. All she had to do was shake it off, like she would shake off a bad hit.

She blinked again then deliberately turned her back to the other end of the ice. She pasted a big smile on her face, ignoring the odd looks from Shannon and Taylor.

"Okay, LeBlanc. Your turn. What's your secret?"

An expression of forced innocence flashed across Taylor's face. "What secret? I don't have a secret."

"Oh, no you don't. That's not even funny. You said you had a secret. Out with it."

Taylor glanced around them, like she was making sure they were alone, then leaned in. Sammie and Shannon moved closer, so all three of their heads were huddled together.

"You have to swear not to tell anyone. And I mean it. You can't breathe a word of this or I will get into so much trouble."

"We won't."

Sammie nodded her agreement, then repeated Shannon's words. "We won't."

"Okay." Taylor took a deep breath, looked around them once more, then leaned in even closer, her voice barely a whisper. "It looks like the exhibition game is really going to happen."

Sammie leaned back, exchanged a look with Shannon, then shook her head. "What exhibition game?"

"Shh!" Taylor grabbed her arm and pulled her closer. "Not so loud. And what do you mean, 'what exhibition game'? You know."

"No, I don't."

"Yes, you do. *The* exhibition game. The one Chuckie was talking about? I told you he was working on it."

"No, you didn't."

"Yes, I did." Taylor frowned, her gaze darting between Shannon and Sammie. "Against the Banners?"

"What!"

"Holy crappola. Are you serious?"

Taylor slapped the palm of her hand against her face and shook her head, groaning. "I can't believe you two. Didn't I tell you to be quiet?"

"We weren't that loud."

"Yes, you were. And how could you not know what I was talking about? I know I mentioned it to both of you already."

"Yeah, but I thought you were joking."

"So did I." Shannon straightened, a speculative gleam in her eyes. "So this is going to be for real? You're seriously not joking?"

"Not at all. I don't have the exact date, but it'll probably be near the end of January. And the Banners are going to be doing a lot of marketing for it, too. This could be really big."

"Oh. My. God." The words fell from Shannon's lips, a sort of awed whisper of disbelief. She said them again, a little louder, then again. Taylor reached out and yanked her arm, silencing her.

"Would you stop? People are starting to look."

Shannon laughed, snapping out of whatever odd stupor had possessed her. "Yeah, so? It's not like they know what we're talking about."

"Maybe not but Chuckie's looking over, too. I don't want him to figure it out."

"Oh, like he doesn't already know? Please, girl. He probably knew you'd spill your guts to us as soon as he told you."

"That doesn't matter. I don't want him figuring it out. Not yet." Taylor waved her hands at each of them in a shooing motion. "So go. Skate around. Go do something before he comes over here."

Sammie exchanged an amused look with Shannon, rolled her eyes, then spun around and took off down the ice. She had planned on doing a few laps, just to stretch her legs and make sure whatever stupid emotions she had felt earlier were truly gone before joining Jon and Clare.

Yes, hearing about the exhibition game—or at least the possibility of it, because she didn't want to get her hopes up until it really happened—had certainly helped. But she still needed to clear her head, to convince herself that it hadn't been jealousy she had felt earlier. She *couldn't* be jealous. There was nothing to be jealous of, because she and Jon weren't together, and they never would be. They *couldn't* be. It was over between them, and she had no desire for a reconciliation.

So what if Shannon and Taylor were convinced otherwise? That was just them being funny.

Wasn't it?

Yes, of course it was.

Sammie finished her second lap and was starting on her third when she looked toward center ice. Jon was standing there, Clare held securely in his arms, pointing toward her.

Watching her.

Even from this distance, she could see the expression in his eyes, feel the intensity of his gaze as heat shot through her.

Pride. Excitement.

Regret.

Need.

Desire.

Oh God, she could *feel* it, feel all of it as he stood there, watching her, holding their daughter in his arms. The look, the force of his emotions, slammed into her, stealing her breath.

She lost her balance, caught the edge of her blade on something—probably her own skate—and went tumbling to the ice, sliding on her backside until she came to an ungraceful stop against the boards.

Right in front of Rachel, who stood there and laughed.

chapter SIXTEEN

"Are you sure you didn't hurt yourself when you fell?"

"Positive." Nothing but her pride, not that she would admit that out loud.

Sammie placed the cups—two hot chocolates and a small plastic cup of ice—on the table then slid onto the bench, moving over to make room for Clare. But her daughter clung to Jon instead, her head resting on his shoulder. He didn't even hesitate, just slid into the booth across from her and readjusted Clare on his lap.

Sammie frowned, tried to ignore the flash of hurt that pierced her. It was a good thing that Clare had bonded so quickly with her father. Right? Yes, of course it was.

Sammie slid back out then leaned over, her hands reaching for Clare's jacket. "Her coat needs to come off, so she doesn't get overheated."

"I've got it." Jon flashed her a smile then unzipped

Clare's jacket, easily sliding the sleeves from her arms. Sammie stood there, feeling like a sudden outcast, as he tossed the jacket beside him and readjusted Clare on his lap. Not that he *needed* to do anything, because Clare willingly settled against him, like she was staking her claim on him and nothing would get in her way.

Sammie frowned again then sat back down, telling herself it meant nothing.

Maybe, if she said it enough times, she'd actually believe it.

She reached for Clare's cup and eased the lid off, blowing on the surface of creamy hot chocolate before taking a small sip. It was still too hot, even though she asked for it to be served warm. She grabbed a few ice cubes and dumped them in, stirring them until they melted, then replaced the lid.

"Ready for your hot chocolate, Boo?"

Clare nodded and reached across the table, her hands outstretched as Sammie handed her the cup. Jon frowned, his hand coming up to hold the bottom of the cup as Clare took it.

"Are you sure it's okay for her to drink? It's not too hot or anything, right? She's not going to burn herself?"

It should have been cute, even adorable, the way Jon sat there, hesitation and concern creasing his face. A doted father, putting his daughter's safety first.

It should have been—but it wasn't. It annoyed her instead, like he was questioning every little thing she did, questioning her ability as a mother. It was that irrational annoyance that made her words come out sharper than she intended.

"I'm positive, Jon. I'm her mother. I'm pretty sure I know what I'm doing."

Jon sat back, his face going carefully blank. He watched her with those dark, intense eyes, completely void of any emotion. Then he blinked, and the vacant mask was gone, replaced by a flash of regret.

"I'm sorry. This is all new. I didn't mean to question you."

Sammie sighed, the irritation leaving her. She ran a hand through her hair then dropped it to her lap, the fingers curling against her palm. "I know. I didn't mean—I'm sorry."

She looked away, unable to meet Jon's gaze, and busied herself by glancing around. They were in the coffee shop at the town center where they had met the other night. The shop was small and cozy, with scattered seating areas nestled around the open space and a gas fireplace along the far wall. Customers lined up at the counter, ordering lattes and hot chocolates as they juggled shopping bags from one hand to the next. Other people, the ones who weren't in a hurry, relaxed in chairs and around tables, taking the time to enjoy their drinks as they sat and talked.

Had it only been four days since Jon had opened up to her? Right here, in the upper-level parking lot? Yes, it had—but it felt like so much longer, like so much had changed in that short amount of time.

No. Impossible. It had only been four days—no, that wasn't right. Four days since they had talked, yes, but only three days since she had taken Clare to see Jon for the first time. Not even three full days, not technically.

She took a sip of her drink and watched the two of them across the table. Jon's head was bent toward his daughter's, tilted to the side as he talked to Clare in low tones. Sammie had no idea what he was saying, but

Clare was enthralled, listening to him with undivided attention, her brown eyes wide and focused on him.

Sammie cleared her throat and leaned forward. "What are you telling her?"

"Hm?" Jon looked up, as if just remembering that Sammie was there. She frowned again. If he noticed, he didn't say anything. "Just talking."

"Yeah?" Sammie tried to smile, tried to make her voice sound light and carefree, like she was only mildly curious. "What about?"

"Nothing. Just daddy stuff."

Sammie stiffened, shot a panicked look at Clare, to see if her daughter had picked up on the word. "Jon—"

"I know. Sorry. It slipped out."

Had it? Or had he done it on purpose? And did it matter? He *was* Clare's father. She didn't plan on hiding that from her, but she wasn't sure how to tell her, had no idea how to even bring it up. She had asked Jon not to say anything, not yet. Not until Sammie was able to figure out the best way to handle things.

If there even *was* a best way. Was she overreacting? Worrying too much? Maybe she should just let things run their natural course, wait to see how Clare handled Jon's sudden presence in her life.

Or maybe not. Looking at Clare now, curled up against Jon, it was obvious she was completely comfortable with him. And from the expression on Jon's face, from the quick flashes of emotion she glimpsed in his eyes, there was no doubt that Clare had him totally and completely wrapped around her little finger.

Sammie offered him a small smile then dropped her gaze to the surface of the wood table. "It's okay.

I'm probably just overreacting."

"Are you sure?"

"Yeah."

"Then why do you look so sad?"

Sammie's head shot up, her eyes narrowing. "I don't look sad."

"Well, no. Not right now. But you did."

"You were seeing things."

"You sure about that?"

"Yeah. Positive."

Jon watched her for several long seconds, his gaze holding hers, refusing to let her look away. Then he shrugged, a small smile teasing the corners of his mouth. Sammie's heart jumped in her chest, stopped, then resumed beating so fast and loud, she was certain Jon must be able to hear it. If he did, it didn't show.

Thank God. Because holy crappola, what had that been about?

"So, tell me about the Blades. How did you get started playing for them?"

The question caught her off-guard but only for a second. Why, she didn't know. It was a harmless question, nothing more than the start of casual conversation. And it was safe, much safer than the hundred other questions he could have asked, the ones she saw lingering just beneath the surface of those dark, intense eyes.

"There was an announcement in the paper for tryouts and I figured, why not? I went and then the next thing I knew, I was on the roster."

"Why do I get the feeling there's a lot more to it than that?"

Sammie smiled. "Maybe. I spent a lot of hours at the rink in Reisterstown trying to get ready. I thought my legs were going to fall off. And I never thought I'd actually make it."

"But you did. Good for you. I'm proud of you."

Warmth spread through her at the heartfelt words. She tried to shrug them off, told herself they shouldn't mean anything—*couldn't* mean anything. But they did, and she wasn't sure why.

"Thanks. But it's only the first season. And there aren't any guarantees we'll be back next year."

"How come?"

"Because it's not a rec league. Because they need to make money. Because ticket sales aren't that great and right now, they *aren't* making money. At least, not a lot. Lots of reasons."

"The stands weren't exactly empty last week when I was there."

"Yeah. But they weren't exactly filled, either."

"Maybe not, but it's only been—what, a couple months?"

"Not even. Our first game was in early October."

"Plenty of time, then. I wouldn't worry about it."

Yeah, that was easy for him to say. Jon didn't understand how much they all had riding on this. Didn't understand that there was no place else for them to go. Some of them—like Taylor and Shannon—were just as good, if not better, than some of the pro players Sammie had seen. And it was so unfair that they didn't have the chance to prove it, to show what they could do, simply because they were women.

Sammie didn't tell him any of that, though. It wasn't that she didn't think he'd understand—she just didn't feel like sharing that much with him yet. Those dreams and hopes and worries.

Jon steadied Clare's cup as she took another sip of

her hot chocolate, then smiled when she shook her head and pushed it away. Clare gave a happy little sigh then snuggled closer to her father, one hand curled around the open V of his thermal Henley. Sammie felt a twinge of something dangerously warm at the sight and forced her gaze away.

"So tell me about that blonde."

Sammie looked up, frowning, then realized he must be talking about one of her teammates. "Which one?"

"Not your friend. The other one, the one who was laughing at you."

The warm feeling evaporated, replaced by an icy chill that went bone-deep. Sammie sat up a little straighter and frowned. "You mean Rachel Woodhouse."

"Is that her name? What's her story?"

"Why? Are you interested?" Sammie wished she could take the words back, wished she had taken just a second to *think* before speaking. It wasn't just the words—it was her tone of voice. Cold. Judgmental.

Jealous.

And Jon knew it, too. She could tell from the way he was looking at her, with that glint of amusement that flashed in his eyes and the faintest hint of a smile that played with one corner of his stupid, sculpted mouth.

"Would you care?"

Yes.

Sammie didn't say that, though. She couldn't—she *didn't* care, she wouldn't *allow* herself to care. And the last thing she needed to do was let Jon think—for even a fraction of a second—that there was even the slightest chance she might care.

She took a careful sip of her drink, silently

composing herself, hoping Jon couldn't see the way her hand tightened around the cup—like the insulated cardboard was Rachel's neck and she was gleefully squeezing it.

She placed the cup back on the table then offered him a sweet smile. "You're a grown man. Who you do is your business."

Jon just sat there, watching her, his brows slightly raised in amusement. A second went by, then two, before Sammie realized what she had said. She yanked her gaze away from Jon's, heat rushing to her face.

"I mean *what*. *What* you do is your business."

"Hm-hmm. Sure."

"I didn't mean—"

"If you say so. Before you jump to more conclusions, I was only asking because she seemed a little…I don't know. Pushy. Forceful. Maybe desperate, even. Like she was trying to prove something."

"Ha. Like Rachel cares about proving anything to anyone. Trust me, Rachel is only worried about herself. Amanda's the same way."

"Who's Amanda?"

"She wasn't there today. I'm not even one hundred percent sure she's still on the team. I mean, I think she is but maybe not."

"What happened?"

"Turns out she was using drugs. She OD'd at one of the games a couple weeks ago so then they tested everyone and they kicked her off the team. Except I think they changed their minds and offered to help her with rehab because Chuckie told them it would be bad PR if they didn't."

"Chuckie?"

"Yeah. He's the head of marketing and PR for the Blades, and he's dating Taylor. Only *he* almost got fired, too. Well, not really. He almost sort of quit because they were going to permanently suspend Taylor because they were dating and—why are you laughing?"

Jon ran a hand across his eyes and shook his head. "No reason."

"You were laughing. Why?"

"Because you still do it."

"Do what?"

"Those little bursts you have."

"I don't know what you're talking about." But she did, and she wished she didn't. She thought she had changed that, thought she had broken that habit. And she had—until Jon showed back up.

"Sure you do. You'll sit there, all quiet and refined, then start talking a mile a minute, like you're making up for all the time you were quiet."

"You're imagining things."

"No, I'm not, and you know it." He leaned back in the seat, readjusted Clare in his lap before dropping a kiss on the top of her head, then looked back at Sammie. The teasing light was gone from his eyes, replaced by a seriousness that made Sammie shift uncomfortably in her own seat.

"I missed that. When I was overseas—"

"Jon—"

"I would just sit there sometimes, close my eyes, imagine hearing your voice. Your laughter. Remember the way you would gesture with your hands when you talked—"

"Jon, don't. Please."

"It's just the truth, Sammie. Why don't you want to hear it?"

"You know why. Because—" She swallowed, shook her head, gazed at the fireplace across the room. "It was your choice, Jon. Not mine. You can't tell me how much you thought about me after doing what you did."

"You know why—"

"I know. And maybe part of me understands. But part of me doesn't. And you don't get to tell me how you thought about me. Okay? I can't—I don't want to hear it."

"Fair enough."

They sat there for several long minutes, neither one of them talking, neither one of them looking at the other. Sammie shifted in her seat, looked down at her watch without really seeing the time.

"It's getting late. I need to get Clare home."

Jon reached across the table, his hand closing around hers. Big. Strong. Rough. But gentle, so gentle. Sammie swallowed against the emotion in her throat, forced herself not to move.

"For what's it worth, I'm not interested."

"What?"

"You asked me earlier if I was interested. In your teammate—"

"It's not my business—"

"The only woman I'm interested in is you."

Her eyes shot to his as a dozen different emotions slammed into her. Anger. Hope. Fear. Resentment. Desire. Need.

More hope.

She shook her head, pulled her hand from his, shook her head again. "No. Don't you dare do that to me. It's not fair."

"It's the truth."

"I don't care. It's not happening. It *can't* happen."

"Why not?"

"*Why not?* How can you even ask me that?" Sammie glanced around, pulled in a deep breath and forced herself to calm down. She leaned closer, lowering her voice. "You walked away, Jon. You turned your back on me. On your daughter. You never gave me a chance to help you. You never gave me a *choice*. How can I trust you not to do the same thing again?"

"Because I learned my lesson the first time."

Sammie sat there, watching him, unable to look away from the gaze holding hers. Dark. Intense. Hypnotizing. Her heart pounded in her chest and her lungs burned with each short, rapid breath. And she realized, in between one heartbeat and the next, that she wanted to believe him.

Oh God, she wanted to believe him.

She closed her eyes, breaking the spell he seemed to hold over her, and shook her head. "I need to leave."

Had she expected him to argue? To put up a fight and try to convince her to stay? To try to change her mind? Not just about leaving but about…everything.

He didn't. He simply nodded and grabbed Clare's jacket, started helping her into it. Sammie slid out from the bench, tried to take Clare from him. "I can do that."

"I've got it."

"I said I can do it—"

"And I said I have it." Jon gave her one last, long look, one she couldn't read, then straightened Clare's coat around her and zipped it up. He stood up, sweeping Clare into his arms with a smooth, efficient, move.

Like he'd been taking care of his daughter for her entire life.

Sammie started to reach for her, needing to feel her daughter's warmth, needing to hold her. But Clare wrapped her arms around Jon's neck and shook her head, her curls bouncing back and forth. "No!"

Sammie blinked, surprised at the sharp command in Clare's voice, surprised at the sharp stab of pain she felt at that single word. She told herself not to read into it, reminded herself that this was part of a normal stage at Clare's age, that making a big deal of it would only make it worse.

But it still hurt.

Sammie forced a smile to her face then turned and led the way out of the coffee shop, the sound of Jon's heavy steps behind her as she walked to her car. She'd been lucky, finding a spot not too far away. She was even more thankful for that luck now, because it meant spending less time in Jon's company.

She needed to get away from him, to put distance between them so she could think. So she could convince herself she had only been imagining things, that she wasn't *feeling* anything. That she didn't *want* anything. She was simply tired and overwhelmed by the hectic pace and events of the last few days. That was it. Nothing more.

She dug her keys from her jacket pocket and hit the remote for the locks, then pulled open the rear door. She turned and reached for Clare, bit back the hurt when her daughter snuggled closer to Jon.

"No! Don't want to go with you."

"Clare, sweetie. Come on. Time to go home."

"No! Want to stay here."

"Clare—"

Jon shifted Clare in his arms, holding her so she had to look at him. "Hey, Little Bits. Don't talk to

Mommy that way."

"But I don't wanna go."

"I know you don't. But you have to."

"No!"

"Hey, none of that. If you act up, Mommy won't let us hang out again. You don't want that to happen, do you?"

Sammie opened her mouth, ready to argue with Jon, ready to tell him that he was making her out to be the bad guy, but she stopped when Clare shook her head, suddenly looking serious.

"Noooo."

"Me either. So why don't I get you buckled in so Mommy can take you home, okay?"

"'Kay."

"That's my girl." Jon pressed a kiss to her cheek then stepped past Sammie, kneeling on the backseat as he got Clare buckled into her car seat. Sammie leaned closer, trying to make out the soft words of their conversation, but all she heard were the quiet murmurs of Jon's voice, followed by Clare's high-pitched giggle.

Jon finally straightened, closing the door then turning to face Sammie. Her body was caged by his, her back pressed against the driver's door. He braced his hands on the car's roof, one on either side of her, so she had nowhere to go.

"I want to see her this week."

"Fine. Call me. We can work something out."

"I want to see you, too."

"Jon—"

"Just until I'm sure I'm not going to screw anything up with Clare. You know, like making sure I don't feed her pizza and beer."

"Oh." He had meant he wanted her to be with

Clare, not that he wanted to actually see her. Of course. How stupid was she to read into it? "Yeah. Sure. That's fine."

"Good."

She expected him to step back, to give her room to open the door so she could climb into the car and start it up and leave. But he didn't step back. Instead, he leaned forward, the heat of his body wrapping around her as he dipped his head toward hers.

Sammie stiffened, tried to turn her head to the side, but she couldn't move, realized she didn't *want* to move. How long had it been since she'd been kissed? Almost three years, the last time she had seen Jon, the day he had left. And she wanted to feel his kiss, wanted to see if it was the way she remembered, prayed that it wasn't.

Then Jon's mouth was on hers and she stopped thinking and just *felt*. The heat of his body pressed against hers. The surprising softness of his lips. The warmth of his mouth as he kissed her.

Gentle. Soothing. Seeking.

Sammie held herself still for the space of a few heartbeats. Frozen. Unsure how to act. Afraid to react. Then she sighed and leaned against him, reached up with her free hand and curling it around the edge of his open coat.

And then he pulled away, ending the kiss as quickly as it began. Sammie sagged against the car door, her lips still tingling from his touch, and tried to focus on the man standing in front of her.

Tried to figure out what had just happened.

"Drive safe." He leaned forward and pressed another kiss against her cheek, just a quick one, then turned and walked away.

It took several minutes before she was coherent enough to open the door, and several more before she was finally able to get the keys in the ignition and start the engine.

She was still trying to convince herself that nothing had happened, that the kiss meant absolutely nothing, that she had only imagined her reaction when she pulled into her driveway twenty-five minutes later.

chapter SEVENTEEN

"Are you okay?"

Sammie looked up from tightening her laces. "Yeah. Fine. Why?"

"Because you've been jittery and distracted ever since you got here." Taylor brought the blade of her stick close to her face, tilting her head to the side as she ran her hand along the tape. Then she turned that same studying look on Sammie. "And your play shows it."

Sammie dropped her gaze, thought about making up some excuse, then decided against it. Taylor was only speaking the truth. Sammie had completely blown two plays, giving New York prime scoring chances. The only reason there weren't any points showing up on the scoreboard was because Rachel had rushed forward to cover her screw-ups.

Both times.

Rachel, of all people.

And the woman hadn't bothered to keep her

irritation to herself, either, making more than one snide comment each time they got back to the bench. Nobody had bothered to contradict her, or tell her to keep quiet, because they all knew Rachel was right.

Sammie had messed up and deserved to be called out. It just galled her that it was being done by Rachel.

"Do you want Coach to switch up the lines?"

It wasn't a question, more of a quiet threat. Sammie swallowed back her irritation—Taylor was their Captain, she had to be focused on making sure the team worked together. Switching up the lines was something the coaching staff did, but there was no doubt in Sammie's mind that Coach Reynolds would listen to any suggestion Taylor made.

"No, I'm good."

"You sure about that?"

"Yeah."

Taylor nodded, rested the stick across her lap, then nudged Sammie in the side with a small smile. "Good. Because that would have totally sucked. Now tell me what's going on."

Sammie almost laughed. Tell her what was going on? They were in the locker room for their first intermission, which was more than halfway over. She didn't have enough time to tell Taylor what was going, not in any detail.

So she shrugged and simply said, "Jon's here. With Clare."

"Yeah. I saw him earlier."

"You did?"

"Duh. It's not like the stands are that big, you know. Or that filled. Of course, I saw him. Besides, you kept turning around to look at the crowd. I figured something was up."

"Oh."

"That's it? *Oh?* Aren't you going to elaborate?"

"I don't even know where to start."

"Okay, how about the basics. Are you guys sleeping together yet?"

"What? God, no. Absolutely not. You're worse than Shannon."

"But you're thinking about it."

"No!"

Taylor leaned back, her brows arched over whiskey-colored eyes. "Really?"

There was so much meaning in that one simple word, in the way she drew it out. Disbelief. Surprise. Knowledge of the inevitable. Sammie sighed and looked away, afraid Taylor would see too much on her face.

"No, I'm not. I can't. That would be—that would be *disastrous*. In more ways than I could even imagine."

"You sure about that? Because you guys have been spending a lot of time together these last two weeks, ever since Thanksgiving weekend."

"No, we haven't. He's met me after practice twice and he's here with Clare tonight. That's not 'spending time together'."

"What about the other times? Because you said he's been spending more time with Clare—which means he's with you, too."

"That doesn't mean anything." At least, that's what Sammie tried to tell herself. The problem was, every single time she saw him, every single minute they spent together, chipped away at her resolve to keep her distance.

It should be easy enough. Jon hadn't even tried to kiss her again. Yes, there were times he seemed to stand too close. Times when his arm brushed against hers, or when their hands touched for just a second too long. But there wasn't anything she could point to and say 'stop doing that', not without sounding like an idiot because he wasn't *doing* anything.

Except driving her crazy.

"Well, maybe you should."

"Should, what?"

"Sleep with him."

"What?" Sammie stared at Taylor, trying to figure out if she was joking or not. No, she wasn't. "Are you crazy? Weren't you the one who said I should tell him to get lost?"

"Yeah, but you haven't."

"He's Clare's father. It's not that easy."

"Or that's just a convenient excuse."

"That is the most ridiculous thing I have ever heard."

"Look at it this way, then: if you sleep with him, maybe you'll get him out of your system and you can move on."

"Absolutely not."

"Hey, maybe he'll be a super-dud and that'll help. You'll never know until you try, right?"

"Trust me, it's not in Jon's nature to be a dud in anything. Especially in—God. No. No, we are not having this discussion. I can't believe—"

"If you could see how red your face is right now." Taylor laughed, the sound turning into a small snort as she started to fall back before catching herself. Sammie glared at her through narrowed eyes, wondering how much trouble she'd get in if she knocked Taylor off the bench.

"You're not funny."

"Yes, I am, and you know it."

"You're not. None of this is, because Jon wants to take Clare home tonight so they can spend all day together tomorrow. He wants to take her to the aquarium."

Taylor's laughter faded. She sat back up, sympathy flashing in her eyes. "Is that what's really bothering you?"

"Yeah. I've never—I've never been away from Clare for that long before."

"What about our road games?"

"That's not the same. I mean, we haven't spent the night on the road, you know? I've always been able to go home and tuck her in, even though she was already asleep, and just watch her if I wanted to. Plus, she was *home*. And I'm there in the morning as soon as she wakes up. But this—this is different."

"So then tell him no."

"I already told him yes." She hadn't meant to, but she had taken one look at the silent pleading in Jon's eyes—the pleading he had tried so hard to hide from her when he brought it up—and heard herself say yes.

"Then tell him you changed your mind."

"I can't. You have no idea how much this means to him." But Sammie did, knew he was somehow trying to convince himself that he wasn't the monster he believed himself to be. No, he hadn't brought up their conversation in his car again, hadn't talked about everything he'd done and or what he believed he'd become. Neither one of them had.

But Sammie knew those thoughts weren't very far from the front of his mind. She could see it in the occasional faraway look he got on his face, in the mingled expression of wonder and doubt that flashed in his eyes whenever he looked at Clare.

"Then I don't know what to tell you, Sammie. Except you need to figure something out and I don't mean while you're out on the ice."

"Yeah. I know."

"Good. Then let's go kick some New York butt." Taylor stood and grabbed Sammie's arm, pulling her to her feet as everyone started lining up to head back to the ice. Coach Reynolds came in, gave them a final last-minute talk to pump them up, then they filed past her.

Sammie hit the ice behind Taylor, following her down to the net with the rest of the line to tap Shannon on the legs before lining up for the puck-drop. Sammie looked to the right, her gaze immediately landing on Jon. He was standing with the rest of the crowd, Clare propped on his hip as he pointed toward her. Sammie couldn't make out what he was saying, not from this distance, but she saw Clare bounce up and down in his arms and clap her tiny little hands together.

"Reigler. I need you here."

Sammie turned back around, her gaze meeting Taylor's. She nodded, forced all thoughts of Jon from her mind, and got into position.

New York won the faceoff, immediately skating the puck into the Blades' defensive zone. Sammie powered through each stride, pushing herself, muscles stretching and burning as she followed and slid into position in front of the net. She leaned forward, swinging her stick from side-to-side, her gaze never leaving the player from New York.

Waiting. Watching.

The woman darted to the left, stopped and moved to the right. It didn't matter, Sammie hadn't been fooled. She moved in, reached out with her stick, and knocked the puck loose before the woman could shoot it.

They followed the puck into the corner, both of them hitting the boards hard enough to shake the glass. Sammie jabbed with her elbow, kicked out with the toe of her skate, dug in with her stick until she got her tape on the puck. She jammed her elbow into the other player's side once more then spun around, moving the puck back to center ice.

She glanced around, passed it to Taylor, followed her down the ice then waited, getting into position, focused on keeping the puck in the zone in case of a rebound—or in case one of the players from New York knocked it loose or gained possession of it. Not that there was much chance of that happening, not right now. Taylor had firm possession as she skated around the net, her gaze scanning the ice as she pulled back with her stick.

New York's goalie slid to the right, her glove hand coming up to block the shot. But Taylor didn't take the shot. Instead, she passed the puck to Dani, who pulled back and sent it flying in, hard and fast.

The red light flashed above the net, immediately followed by the sound of the horn blaring. Cheers and applause echoed around them, still not loud enough to drown out the horn, but louder than it had been at every other game so far this season.

Sammie ran forward, meeting Taylor and Dani and Rachel and Sydney for a group hug before heading off the ice. She dropped to the bench and grabbed a water bottle, shooting a stream into her mouth before handing the bottle to Taylor.

Taylor took a quick sip, swished it around her mouth, then leaned to the side and spit it out before taking another sip, swallowing it this time. She tossed the bottle behind her then nudged Sammie in the side.

"See what happens when you aren't distracted and get your head in the game?"

"Hm." Sammie didn't say anything more than that little sound. She couldn't—if she did, Taylor would figure out the truth.

Her head hadn't been in the game, not exactly. Not the way Taylor had meant.

Her mind had been on Jon. On impressing him.

And on her earlier conversation with Taylor, thinking about what she had said, wondering if maybe her friend had a point. Wondering if maybe she *should* just sleep with him and get it out of her system.

Not that she would. There was no way she could allow that to happen, not in real life. But as far as lighting a fire under her during the game—yeah, it had definitely worked.

And it kept working for the rest of the game, too, right up until the final horn signaled another win for the Blades.

chapter
EIGHTEEN

Jonathan shifted Clare in his arms, trying not to disturb her as he jammed the key into the door and unlocked it. He pushed it open then stepped to the side, waiting for Sammie to move past him before closing it again.

"I could have carried her, you know."

"You've already got your hands full." And she did, with a large backpack, Clare's small backpack, and a huge tote bag filled with who-knew-what. It didn't matter that *he* could have carried the bags—and probably should have, since they were probably heavier. But he couldn't pass up the chance to hold Clare in his arms, to feel her small arms wrapped around his neck as she curled against. Warm. Trusting.

And right now, heavier than he thought. She was still sound asleep, had been since they left the restaurant where they had gone to eat after Sammie's game.

Sammie shot him a look that told him she knew his real motive for carrying Clare but she didn't say anything, just moved into the living room and dropped the bags next to the sofa. She looked around, her brows lifted in surprise.

"You've done some decorating."

"Not much. Well, just a little." A few pictures. A fake plant—because he had no idea how to take care of a real one. A soft throw tossed over the back of the sofa, along with some colorful throw pillows. Those had been Mac's idea, something Jonathan still didn't understand.

"It looks nice. Cozy."

Okay, maybe he didn't need to understand. He'd be damned if he admitted that to Mac, though.

He tossed the keys onto the small table by the door then moved further inside, still holding Clare in his arms. "I, uh, I tried to baby proof everything. You know, plugs in the sockets and all that sh—stuff. I didn't know if you wanted to look around and check things out, see if I forgot something."

Amusement flashed in Sammie's eyes as she nodded and made her way around the living room, bending down to check things. He followed her into the dining room then the kitchen, watched as she checked the latches on the cabinets—which were a colossal pain in his ass. He didn't care, though, not if made Clare safer.

And not if helped set Sammie's mind at ease.

She was nervous, he could tell just by looking at her. She tried not to show it, tried to pretend this wasn't bothering her, but he knew it was.

Hell, she wasn't the only one nervous. This was a big step—for both of them. He still couldn't believe she had agreed to let Clare spend the night here. And part of him was terrified that he'd do something wrong, that he'd screw something up.

He moved past Sammie into the hallway, hitting the light switch with his elbow as he went. "I got her a bed too. With those rail things, so she doesn't climb out."

"Rails won't stop her."

Dread filled him and he spun around to face Sammie. "But I thought—"

"They're to keep her from falling out while she's sleeping, but she doesn't really need them. As for climbing—she started climbing out of her crib when she was fifteen months old."

"Oh. Is that normal?"

"It was for her."

"Did you want to see the bed anyway? Just to make sure it's okay?"

"I'm sure it's fine, Jon. But yeah, lead the way."

He nodded and walked down the hall, stopped to push open the door to the second bedroom. It used to be his office, until a few days ago. Now his desk and computer were jammed into his own bedroom, and his former office had been transformed into a room fit for a princess.

Kind of.

He flipped the switch on the wall and soft light filled the room, coming from the pink-and-white lamp resting on the wooden dresser. A child-sized rocking chair made from the same pale wood as the dresser rested in the corner, surrounded by a battalion of stuffed animals. A matching bed, miniature-sized, was placed against the wall, covered in a bright pink camouflage comforter with matching pillowcases.

"What do you think? Is this okay?" He turned to Sammie, anxious to see what she thought. She covered her mouth with one hand, but not before he saw the smile spreading across her face.

"Is it that bad?"

"No." She shook her head, still smiling. "No, it's not bad. It's just—pink camo?"

"Um, I wasn't sure what else to get. Everything was either pink with princesses and unicorns or blue with spaceships and sports stuff. I couldn't find any hockey stuff, or I would have bought that. And I wasn't sure about the whole princess thing so—" He stopped rambling, wondering if he sounded as nervous as he felt. "I can take it back, it's not a big deal."

"It's fine, Jon. Really. I'm sure she'll like it."

Relief swept through him. Maybe Sammie was stretching the truth just a little bit, but she seemed to be okay with it so he wouldn't let himself worry about it.

Not too much, anyway.

He followed Sammie back into the living room then stood there, not sure what to do next. She looked like she was torn between leaving and staying, like she was maybe having second thoughts about this whole thing. He couldn't blame her, not really. Yes, he was Clare's father—but he'd been out of their lives for so long, had totally fucked everything up.

What if he fucked this up, too?

"Did you want anything to drink? A soda or coffee or—"

"No, I should probably get going."

"Are you sure? Because—"

"I'm sure. It'll be easier—" She stopped, looked away and cleared her throat. Jonathan didn't miss the sudden moisture welling in her eyes, even though she tried to hide it. He didn't think, just closed the distance between them and ran his hand along her arm.

"Thank you. For letting her stay."

Sammie nodded, stepped back, hesitated as she looked at Clare, still sleeping in his arms. "I wouldn't let her sleep too long, or she'll never get to sleep tonight. And make sure she brushes her teeth—you'll need to help her with that—and nothing to drink too late. And make sure you put her in her pull-ups before bed."

"I know. You have everything written down for me."

Sammie nodded, took another step toward the door, stopped again. "And you have my number so don't be afraid to call me. Even if it's the middle of the night."

"I know."

"Okay." She nodded, hesitated, nodded again and moved closer to the door. Jon followed her, surprised at the small knot of fear lodged in his gut.

"Don't you want to say goodbye to Clare?" He started nudging Clare, shifting her in his arms so Sammie could kiss her goodbye. Except Sammie was shaking her head, a look of panic on her face.

"Hey, Little Bits. Do you want to say goodbye to Mommy?"

"Jon, I wouldn't do that—"

But Clare had already roused from her sleep and was looking around, confusion marring her face. Her sleepy eyes met his, looked away as she turned toward Sammie and saw her near the door—

And promptly had a meltdown of epic proportions, kicking and screaming and reaching for

Sammie.

Jon tightened his grip on her, honestly worried that she'd thrash her way right out of his arms, she was kicking so hard. He looked at Sammie, desperate for help, totally unsure what to do.

Sammie rushed forward, catching Clare as the little girl lunged toward her. Jon stood there, feeling empty and lost and—

And guilty.

He knew it was an illogical reaction, knew he had nothing to feel guilty for—at least, he didn't think so. Had he done something for Clare to act this way? Could she somehow sense—

No, of course not. He was being an ass. Logically, he *knew* that. But emotionally, deep down where the demons still dwelt, he wasn't so sure.

Could Sammie tell? Maybe. She moved closer, Clare clinging to her like a lifeline, and reached for his hand, her fingers threading with his. "It's not you, Jon. Okay? I knew this might happen."

"But what happened? What did I do wrong?"

"Nothing. You did absolutely nothing wrong. I think it's just separation anxiety."

"What?"

"Separation anxiety. She started to do the same thing the other week, after we went for hot chocolate. Remember?"

He stared down at his crying daughter, watched as tears streamed down her flushed and sweaty face, and shook his head. Clare had never acted like this before.

"When we were leaving, and she said she didn't want to go with me. Remember?"

"But she didn't act like this."

"Not this bad, no, but she was on the verge. Until

you calmed her down." Sammie tightened her hand around his and led him toward the sofa, pulling him down next to her and settling Clare more comfortably against her. The screams had ceased, the crying no longer sounding as desperate.

A strange emptiness filled him when Sammie released his hand to rub gentle circles on Clare's back. And didn't that make him a selfish ass? What kind of man would begrudge his own daughter her mother's touch?

He shifted on the sofa, putting distance between them, and watched as Sammie comforted his daughter. "Maybe this wasn't such a good idea."

"She'll be fine. Just give her a few minutes to calm down, and we'll try again."

"Try again?" Jonathan didn't try to hide his surprise—or his fear. "You want to put her through this again? No. I can't."

"It's just a stage, Jon. And before you get the wrong idea, no, it isn't easy to walk away. It hurts, more than you can imagine. Trust me." Sammie's voice cracked, breaking something inside him.

"No. No way in hell. I'm not—"

"It doesn't last long. A few minutes. I probably should have just left."

"She—does she do this a lot?"

"It's happened a few times this past month. When I've left for work. Or for a game or practice. Like I said, it's a stage."

"Then maybe we should wait. She doesn't have to stay here. I can pick her up tomorrow morning." There was no way Jonathan could handle seeing his daughter go through that again, whether it was a stage or not. Yes, Clare was already calming down, the tears drying on her face as she watched him with those big brown eyes so much like her mother's.

Sammie didn't seem to hear him. Or if she did, she chose to ignore him, because she shifted Clare to his lap then leaned down and dropped a quick kiss on the top of her head.

"You be a good girl, and I'll see you tomorrow, okay?"

Clare nodded then snuggled against Jonathan, her gaze focused on Sammie as she stood and headed for the door. Jonathan tensed, holding his breath, watching as Sammie moved away. She reached out, grabbed the door handle and—

Clare started crying again, reaching out with her small arms as she called for "Mommy" over and over again. And oh God, it looked like Sammie was going to open the door and walk out, despite the tears in her own eyes.

Desperate fear gripped him and he shot off the sofa, his arms tight around Clare as he hurried to the door. "Sammie. Wait. Don't. I can't do this."

Maybe that made him a coward—hell, that wouldn't surprise him—but he didn't care. He couldn't put Clare through this. And he couldn't put Sammie through this because he could see how much it was tearing her apart too, even though she was trying so hard to hide it.

And he couldn't put himself through this, couldn't be responsible for causing Sammie and Clare more pain. Hadn't he put them through enough hell already?

Jonathan reached out and grabbed Sammie's hand, his grip desperate as he pulled her closer. "Please. Don't. I can't do this."

Sammi blinked away her own tears and stepped

closer, squeezing his hand but not letting it go as she reached out with her free one and brushed the curls from Clare's face. "Sweetie, you're making Daddy sad. Don't you want to stay with Daddy?"

Jonathan froze, Sammie's words echoing in his ears. No, he hadn't heard her right. It was nothing more than wishful thinking. Nothing more than a slip on her part. His lungs burned from lack of air; he unfroze long enough to pull in a shaky breath, his gaze shooting to Sammie's.

No, he hadn't been hearing things. And if it had been a slip, Sammie seemed to be aware of it. He searched her gaze, waiting to see regret in her wide eyes, but there was none.

She looked away, studying Clare as she rubbed her back, her soft voice barely audible over Clare's sniffling tears. "You are. It's stupid not to say it."

"I—" Jonathan swallowed, cleared his throat, swallowed again. "Thank you."

Sammie shrugged, her gaze darting to his then sliding away. A small flush stained her cheeks, reminding him of how easy it used to be to embarrass her. How he would tease her when they were younger, just to get that same reaction from her.

And then, when they were older, how he could do other things to make that same flush appear on her round cheeks.

Jonathan placed Clare in Sammie's arms and quickly stepped away, needing to put distance between them before he did something stupid. He moved over to the sofa, leaned down to grab the bags Sammie had dropped there earlier, and tossed them over his shoulder. "I'll help you load up."

"But I thought—"

"It's too soon. I was rushing things. Clare isn't ready. I don't think I am, either."

Sammie stood there, holding his daughter in her arms. Madonna and child, he thought. Innocent. Sweet. And deserving so much more than what he could ever give them. Hadn't he fucked up enough? He should have never come back. If he were smart, he'd walk Sammie to her car and tell her goodbye, and never see her again.

But fuck, he wasn't smart. He was a fucking selfish bastard because he wanted Sammie back. He wanted Clare. He wanted both of them, even though he didn't deserve either one of them.

"I think you are. You just have to be patient and give it time."

Was Sammie talking about Clare? Or something else? Christ, he wanted to think she was talking about something else—about her, about them—but he was afraid to read too much into it. Afraid to hope.

He started to shake his head, only to stop when Sammie pushed past him and headed back to the sofa. She sat on the end of it and yanked the soft throw from the back, spreading it down then sitting Clare next to her. She wrapped the throw around Clare then nodded toward one of the bags hanging from his shoulder.

"There are some movies in that tote bag. Put one in then come have a seat." She patted the sofa next to Clare, a silent dare in her eyes. Jonathan hesitated, still afraid to move, still afraid he was imagining things.

Sammie rolled her eyes then leaned over to Clare, who looked like she had made a complete recovery—again. "Boo, tell Daddy we want to watch a movie."

A big smile blossomed on Clare's face as she bounced up and down. "Watch a movie, Daddy. Now."

The air rushed from his lungs, leaving him reeling and gasping for breath. He swallowed, his gaze searching Sammie's. The understanding he saw in her eyes nearly did him in. It took more strength than he realized not to collapse into a worthless heap right there.

No, he wouldn't do that, not with Sammie and Clare watching him. Waiting.

He sucked in a deep breath and pulled his gaze from Sammie's, dug through the tote bag until his hand closed over the plastic case of a movie. He placed the bags on the floor, the world slowly shifting until the sense of unreality twisted and straightened and became reality.

He sucked in a deep breath, a hesitant smile crossing his face. "I guess we're watching a movie, huh?"

Chapter NINETEEN

Sammie leaned over the bed, gently running one hand through Clare's thick curls. Clare shifted in her sleep, uttered a sleepy mumble, then curled onto her side, one tiny arm wrapped around the fluffy stuffed bear.

Something in his chest squeezed tight, making it hard to breathe, affecting his lungs and heart and even his vision as he stared at his daughter clutching the bear. He remembered when he bought it, nothing more than a last-minute gift he had seen at the PX on his way to pick up Sammie and Clare from the hospital. He remembered walking—no, he'd been *strutting*, every inch the proud father—into Sammie's room, carrying her small bag because he'd been so frazzled he had forgotten to throw it in the car when she went into labor. He held the bear in one hand, laughing when Sammie's eyes widened.

"Jon! That thing is bigger than she is!"

"So she'll grow into it." He leaned over, brushed his lips against the top of Clare's head, feeling the downy softness of the baby-fuzz that covered her scalp. Then he leaned up and claimed Sammie's mouth, this kiss much more than a brushing of lips.

Sammie pulled away, an enchanting blush staining her round cheeks, chasing away some of the exhaustion that had put dark circles under her eyes. The labor hadn't been easy or quick, and weakness still threatened to cut him off at the knees when he thought about it, thought about how helpless he had felt, unable to do anything except hold Sammie's hands and whisper soft words of encouragement in her ear.

He reached for Clare, his hands shaking as he pulled her tiny little body into his arms. She was perfect, just like her mother. Dark blue eyes, already showing a hint of brown—at least, he thought so. Chubby round face. Ten tiny perfect fingers and ten tiny perfect toes.

Perfect. Just like her mother.

Jonathan blinked against the memory, rubbed at the tightness spreading through his chest. Had he forgotten that day, just over three years ago? No, never. But he had shoved it deep into the back of his mind, afraid of pulling it out, afraid of remembering.

They'd been so happy back then, even as they stumbled through each day, trying to figure out that thing called parenthood. Reconnecting with each other as they enjoyed each new little milestone as it happened. Clare's first bath. First smile. First coo. The first time she lifted her head. And the first time she slept through the night, scaring the hell out of both of them.

And then he received his orders to ship out for the second time. They had both known it was coming, had both tried to prepare for it.

But leaving them had nearly killed him. Saying

goodbye, seeing Sammie's eyes fill with sadness and fear while she held Clare and that big fuzzy bear in her arms…fuck. Seeing that had torn him apart. Had he known even then that something would happen?

Maybe.

And then—

Jonathan shook his head, forced his mind to the present as he watched Sammie ease away from Clare. His wife and daughter.

Except Sammie wasn't his wife, not anymore.

And he hadn't been a part of Clare's life since that day he'd left them standing on the porch of their small house, almost three years ago.

He stepped away from the doorway to let Sammie pass, watched as she pulled the door closed behind her, leaving it open just a few inches. Jonathan followed her down the hallway to the living room, watched as she crossed her arms in front of her. Her eyes met his, darted away and focused on something just over his shoulder.

"She usually sleeps through the night but you should keep an ear out, just in case."

"I'm a pretty light sleeper." The answer was automatic, the words leaving him before his mind really registered what Sammie had said. He stepped closer, frowning. "Wait. Are you leaving?"

"I should. It's getting late."

"But—" Jonathan cleared his throat, trying to tamp down the panic. It wasn't just panic. He didn't want Sammie to leave, not yet. "How about some coffee?"

"I don't—"

"Or maybe you should run through that list again. What if she wakes up crying, asking for you?"

"Then you hold her and read her a story until she calms down."

"What about—"

"Jon." Sammie stepped closer, placed a hand on his arm and squeezed. "You'll be fine, okay?"

He shook his head, needing to tell her no, he wouldn't be fine. Needing to tell her that he was scared shitless. Needing to confess every single doubt and worry and fear.

Needing *her*.

Desire slammed into him. Hot. Desperate. Not just desire—*need*. Bone-deep and frantic and so powerful his legs nearly buckled from the force of it. He swallowed, tore his gaze away from Sammie's hand, and looked up.

She was standing there, an odd expression on her face as she watched him with wide eyes. She started to move her hand, started to back away. He wrapped an arm around her waist, holding her in place.

"Stay." Just a single word, filled with raw need.

"I can't. This—" Her tongue darted out, swiped against her lower lip. "This is a bad idea, Jon."

"Please."

He held his breath, waiting, expecting her to pull away. But Sammie didn't move, didn't even blink as she stared up at him with those deep, brown eyes. He tightened his hold, pulled her closer, his eyes never leaving hers.

Waiting for her to push against him and run out the door.

Praying she wouldn't.

He lowered his head, slow, inch by inch, giving her time to pull away. To tell him to stop. Watching. Waiting. And then his lips brushed against hers. Once.

Twice. The touch featherlight, nothing more than a gentle grazing of flesh against flesh.

He heard her swift intake of breath, felt her stiffen for the briefest second—

And then she moved toward him, her arms wrapping around his neck as she pressed her body closer, warm, soft curves against hard flesh.

Jonathan held her close, his mouth claiming hers with a need so desperate, his entire body shook. He ran his tongue along the seam of her lips, groaned when her mouth opened under his.

And fuck. She was everything he remembered and more. Sweet. Spicy. Tantalizing. Intoxicating. Had he forgotten her taste? Her touch? He hadn't thought so. It had been those memories that had carried him through too many dark nights to count.

But the memories didn't even come close to reality. He realized that now, as Sammie clung to him, her hands twisting the thin material of his shirt. He deepened the kiss and tightened his hold on her, needing her even closer. Needing to feel more of her, to become one with her.

His fingers trembled as he trailed his hands up her back, fear accompanying the need. And God, he needed her. More than air. More than life. But it had been so long—for him, for them. Too long. Would she shy away from his touch? Push him away as hate and loathing at all the things he'd done filled her eyes?

What if she didn't push him away but he still somehow managed to fuck things up? Things were different between them now—there was no *them*, thanks to him. They had both changed, become different people. What if—

Sammie sighed into his mouth, the sound a

breathy moan of need that gave him courage. Gave him hope. He dragged his hands through her hair, the silky tendrils soft against his fingers, and cupped the sides of her face. Tilted her head back, deepened the kiss.

Sammie's hands dug into his arms, her fingers kneading the flesh of his biceps as she moved even closer, her hips slowly rocking against his. And fuck, she felt so good. So soft and warm against the rock-hard length of his erection.

Jonathan dragged his mouth from hers, gently teased her lower lip with his teeth before trailing kisses along her jaw and throat. Up to that sensitive spot behind her ear and across her damp cheek—

He pulled away, regret slicing through him when he saw the tears on her face. He dropped his hands, stepped back, his blood turning to ice. "God. Sammie. I'm sorry. I didn't—"

The words caught in his throat, nearly choking him. He raised his hand, needing to soothe her, reassure her. He let it drop as hopelessness and despair washed over him.

"Sammie. Please, babe, don't cry. I'm sorry. I didn't mean—"

"I'm not crying." She stepped closer, ran the palm of her hand up his arm and across his chest, until it was resting against his racing heart. Tears glistened in her eyes as she watched him with an intensity that seared his soul.

Jonathan's chest heaved with the force of the breath he sucked in. He raised one hand and cupped her cheek, wiped away a falling tear with his thumb. "I didn't mean to hurt you."

Did he mean then—or now? Both. But he

couldn't find the words, didn't know how to tell her he was sorry, so fucking sorry—

Sammie caught his hand with hers, pulled it away then turned her head to the side and pressed a lingering kiss against his palm. Fire danced across the roughened skin, tiny flames that traveled up his body, threatening to engulf him. Consume him.

Jonathan swallowed past the lump in his throat, curled his fingers around hers. "Why are you crying, babe?"

Sammie's only answer was a small shake of her head. He opened his mouth, ready to ask again, so fucking worried that he'd done something wrong, so worried that he had fucked up again—

The words died in his throat when Sammie dropped his hand and stepped closer, her gaze searing him as much as her kiss had. She reached between them, grasped the hem of his shirt, and slowly pushed it up. The palms of her hands grazed his skin—the flat plane of his stomach, the breadth of his ribs, the width of his chest. The beat of his heart echoed in the still air around them. Blood pounded through his veins, slow and heavy, hot. Sammie pushed the shirt higher, nudging his arms up. He grabbed the shirt, yanked it over his head, tossed it to the floor.

Then he just stood there, afraid to move. Powerless to move. Sammie's gaze drifted over him, the gaze followed by the hesitant touch of her hand. Across his shoulders, lower, tracing the bold lines of the tattoo emblazoned on his left chest and the scar that ran across his ribs. Her eyes darted to his, filled with silent questions. Jonathan shook his head, unable to answer. He couldn't speak. Hell, he could barely breathe, not with the way she was studying him, not with the way her trembling fingers touched him, so soft and hesitant.

Like she was relearning his body. Like she was seeing him for the first time.

And in a way, she was.

She moved around him. Touching, always touching. The tense muscles of his arms and shoulders. The back of his neck. The groove of his spine, down to the waistband of his jeans and back up again. Jonathan's breath left him with a sharp hiss. He clenched his jaw, closed his eyes as his head dropped back, just...feeling. Feeling each little touch, so afraid to move as Sammie circled him. Still moving, touching, her trembling fingers sending flames dancing across his skin.

She traced the outline of his ribs, his side, back to his chest as she completed a full circle. Still touching, always touching.

And then she pressed her mouth against his chest, above his heart, the kiss light and tender and gentle. The breath left him in a rush. He dropped his head, forced his eyes open, and tumbled into the depths of need filling her watery gaze.

"I need you to touch me, Jon. Please."

chapter TWENTY

I need you to touch me, Jon. Please.

The words rang in his ears. But they were more than words—they were a plea, uttered in a soft voice that drifted through his mind, touching him in places he'd thought long dead.

And they terrified him.

Jonathan held himself still, afraid to move, afraid to do as she asked. So fucking afraid he'd do something wrong. Could Sammie sense the fear gripping him? She reached up, traced the outline of his mouth with the tip of one finger, then ran that same finger across his jaw, over his chin, down his arm. She curled her hand around his and brought it to her mouth, her eyes never leaving his as she pressed another gentle kiss against his palm. There was something about the way she placed that gentle kiss, something about the way she was looking at him—

The paralyzing fear left him, disappearing with the

doubts and worries and regrets that had held him in place. He cupped the side of her face with one hand, trailed the other along her side, down to her hip. He curled on finger through the belt loop of her jeans and tugged, pulling her closer. His dipped his head, claimed her mouth in a searing kiss that left him breathless.

She clung to him, soft little sighs of need escaping from her mouth into his. He deepened the kiss, swirled his tongue against hers. Tasting. Claiming. Demanding.

He reached between them, his fingers thick and clumsy as they worked the buttons of her shirt, taking minutes to do what should have been accomplished in seconds. He pushed the shirt off her shoulders, heard the soft hiss of material as it fell from her arms. And God, she was warm, so soft and warm. He broke the kiss, the sounds of harsh breathing filled the air. His. Hers. Mingling together, an echo of need. Of desire.

He drank her in, feasting on the sight of pale skin tinged with the faintest of blushes. The column of her graceful neck, the pulse beating fast and heavy against soft flesh. The slope of her shoulders, the lean lines of her toned arms.

The flushed skin of firm breasts pushing against soft cotton, rising and falling with each short breath. Jonathan swallowed past the desperate need filling him and reached out with both hands, tracing the straps of the bra. Down, then up. Down again, his knuckles grazing the gentle swell of flesh. The flush coloring her skin deepened. Her breath rushed out in a small gasp as he reached behind her and undid the hooks of the bra and gently eased it off her.

And fuck, she was beautiful, so fucking beautiful that it took his breath away, that it almost hurt to look at her. He ran his tongue along his lips, swallowed against the sudden dryness in his throat.

He needed to tell her how beautiful she was, needed to tell her a million different things, but he couldn't get the words out, not with the way his throat was closing up. Could he show her?

Yes. At least, he could try.

He ran the backs of his hands along her shoulders, reveling in the feel of warm, bare skin. Lower, slow, so slow, grazing his knuckles along the gentle swell of her bare breasts, finally cupping each one in his hands. He circled each nipple with his thumbs, watched as the dusky peaks tightened under his touch. Sammie gasped, her head dropping back, the movement pushing her breasts more fully against him.

Jon bent down, closed his mouth over one tight peak, and pulled. Sucking, licking, gently nipping. She gasped again, the sound a low, keening wail, and dug her nails into the flesh of his arms. One hand wrapped around the back of his head, pulling him closer.

Holding him in place.

Jonathan wrapped one arm around her waist, supporting her as she leaned back. He pulled harder on her nipple, the peak hot and hard and tight against his tongue. Her hips rocked, not quite meeting his as she whispered his name in a breathy moan.

Jonathan swirled his tongue around the tight peak one last time then released it, leaning up to capture her mouth with his in time to swallow her sigh. He bent down, caught her behind the legs, and swooped her into his arms, deepening the kiss as he carried her to his room.

He nudged the door closed, carried her over to the bed and followed her down to the mattress, still kissing her. Touching her, his hands roaming along bare flesh, skimming the denim covering her legs.

He pulled away, his hands shaking as he reached for the button and zipper of her jeans. Sammie nudged his hands away and pushed the jeans over her hips, pausing long enough to kick off her shoes before shoving the denim down and off. She looked up at him, her gaze a gut-wrenching contradiction of shyness and need.

And a reflection of the same desperate hunger coursing through him.

Jonathan fell on her, bracing the bulk of his weight on his elbows as his mouth crashed against hers. Hotter. Harder. Demanding her full surrender, giving his own in return.

She wrapped her legs around his waist, rocked her hips against the length of his cock. Her hands grazed his back, her fingers kneading, sliding across his slick flesh, drifting down into the waistband of his jeans. And fuck, if she didn't stop moving like that, didn't stop rocking against him—

She reached between them, undid the button of his jeans, fought with the zipper, her knuckles grazing his cock through the denim. Jonathan tore his mouth from hers, fighting to breathe, and grabbed her wrist.

To stop her? To turn her hand so she could cup his length through the denim?

Both. Neither. He didn't care, was beyond caring. He just wanted her. Needed her.

More than he'd ever needed her before.

Now.

Forever.

He eased her legs from his waist, rolled off the bed and to his feet in one quick move, and shoved his jeans and briefs down and off. Then he was back on top of her again, losing himself in the feel of warm flesh against warm flesh as he stretched his body along the length of her own.

Sammie's arms closed around him, her mouth seeking his, her teeth nipping at his lips before her tongue darted in to dance with his. She dragged a foot up along his calf, his thigh. Draped it around his hips and pulled him closer, rubbing herself against his straining, throbbing cock. And fuck, he wanted to plunge into her. Lose himself.

Find himself.

The only thing stopping him from driving into her was the cotton fabric of her skimpy underwear. Jonathan reached between them, dipped his hand beneath the elastic, stroked her clit with one trembling finger. And fuck, she was so hot. So wet.

Sammie sighed into his mouth, the sound long and low as she raised her hips and rocked against his touch. He stroked her again, harder, finding the exact spot where she liked to be touched.

She moaned, rocked her hips faster, her nails digging into his arms.

Jonathan slid his hand away, grabbed the cotton and yanked it off her legs, the sound of elastic snapping and breaking lost in the sound of Sammie's frantic cry. And then he was touching her again, stroking her clit. Harder. Faster. His touch matching the rhythm of her harsh, rapid breathing.

He deepened the kiss. Possessing. Claiming. He grabbed one of her hands and stretched her arm over her head, then slid one long finger inside her.

Her back arched as she ripped her mouth from his, calling his name in a harsh breath as her body shattered. Jonathan shifted, the tip of his cock teasing her wet heat. He shifted once more, closed his hand around her hips to keep her still, and drove into her.

Tight. Hot. Wet.

Fuck. Had it always been this way?

He rocked into her, thrusting hard. Held himself still as her body tightened around him. Pulled back and drove himself deep once more. Over and over. Harder. Faster.

Marveling at the way her snug body fit around his. In the way she clung to him, pulling him even deeper.

Realizing his memories hadn't even come close to this. Wondering how he could have forgotten the breathy little moans she made, the way her back arched and the way her head tilted back. The way she bit down on her lower lip as her legs tightened around his waist.

And then he thought no more, just lost himself in the wonder of Sammie's body welcoming his, as if they had never been apart.

chapter
TWENTY-ONE

Shadows filled the room, the darkness held at bay by the pale light streaming in through the part in the curtains. Sammie could just make out the faint sound of the wind, knew the night air outside would be cold. Frigid.

But here, curled next to Jon, she was warm. Safe. Protected.

That's what she wanted to believe, but she knew it was just an illusion. A fantasy.

And a dangerous one at that.

But she didn't move. Didn't jump from the bed and run from the room. Didn't cower under the covers or hide her head under the pillow. Dangerous fantasy or not, this is where she wanted to be.

Curled up against Jon's side, his arm draped around her, her head cradled in the hollow of his shoulder. Her hand rested in the middle of his chest, the steady *thump-thump-thump* of his heart beating beneath her palm somehow calming. Reassuring.

How many times had they fallen asleep like this? With their legs entwined, their bodies pressed so close together she didn't know where she ended and he began? So many times. All her life, it seemed.

And God, she had missed it. Missed it so much. His touch. His warmth. The sound of his breathing and the feel of his callused palm drifting across her back, lulling her to sleep.

The intimacy of just *being*, of knowing she was part of something bigger than just herself.

How many times in the last two years had she awakened in the middle of the night, reaching across the narrow double bed, searching for that missing connection? How many times had that vast sense of loneliness nearly overwhelmed her when she realized she was alone?

Too many nights.

She had tried so hard to forget how this felt, had tried so hard to convince herself she didn't *need*, didn't *want*. But those empty words had been nothing but lies meant to console the aching loneliness deep inside her.

And it would be easy, so easy, to stay here in Jon's arms. In his bed. To stay with *him*. To lose herself in the comfort of his arms, in the intimacy of his touch. Not in sex—though it would be so easy to lose herself in that as well—but in just *being* with him.

But she couldn't. That would be nothing but a mistake, one that wouldn't solve anything—if there was even anything to solve.

That didn't mean she regretted sleeping with him—having sex with him. Sammie knew she should. And maybe she would, tomorrow or next week or next month. But she didn't. She couldn't. It had been something they both wanted, something she had needed.

Maybe that made her a fool. If that was the case, then so be it.

Jon's hand moved, tracing small circles along her back before drifting up and tangling in the short strands of her hair. Soothing. Relaxing. His chest rose and fell with a deep breath, the gravelly whisper of his voice rumbling in her ear.

"You should get some sleep."

"So should you."

"I'm fine."

Was he? There was something about his voice, too low and too quiet, that contradicted the words. Had his thoughts gone down the same road as hers, remembering how things used to be between them? Or were his thoughts haunted by something deeper? By memories she couldn't imagine and images she was afraid to picture?

Sammie shifted, pushing up on her elbow. The room was too dark for her to clearly see his face, to make out the expression in his eyes. But she knew he was looking at her, felt the strength of his gaze as he watched her.

His hand drifted along her neck, his fingers tracing the outline of her jaw. Her lips. Her cheek. He brushed the wayward strands of hair from her face and tucked them behind her ear, his touch soft and gentle.

"I never stopped loving you, Sammie."

The words hit her like a punch to the throat, robbing her of breath. Of reason. Of thought.

No, not of thought—she was thinking plenty, enough to send her into a tailspin of panic. She pushed away from him, heard his muttered curse as his hand dropped to the mattress.

"Sammie—"

"No. You can't say that. You don't get to say that." She swung her legs over the side of the bed, fighting with the tangle of covers and nearly tripping in her haste to get away from him. A light came on behind her, the glare making her squint. She spun around, feeling raw and exposed, the sensation having nothing to do with her lack of clothes.

Jon stood on the other side of the bed, his face carefully blank of all expression—except for his eyes. She could see plenty in their brown depths. Annoyance. Frustration. Confusion. Hurt.

And then he blinked and even his eyes became empty, void of all emotion as he stared at her.

"You don't get to tell me what I feel."

"Yeah, Jon, I do. This—" She motioned at the bed, at the mussed covers still holding the scent of their mixed bodies. "This doesn't mean anything. It just…it just happened. That was all. It doesn't mean anything."

"It doesn't mean anything?" He repeated the words, his voice showing the first hint of emotion.

"No." She crossed her arms over her bare breasts, feeling even more vulnerable as he kept staring at her. But his gaze was focused on her eyes, nowhere else.

Somehow, that was even worse.

"What we just did—" She cleared her throat, ran her tongue across her dry lips and forced the words out. "That was just sex—"

"Don't even go there. It wasn't just sex and you know it."

"It was." And God, she was such a liar. A coward. Could Jon see her real thoughts? Could he see how much it cost her to hide the truth? "It can't be more than that."

He was quiet for several long minutes, the silence in the room stretching around them, growing so thick and heavy, it threatened to suffocate her. He finally moved, breaking the awful tension as he stepped around the bed, coming closer.

But he didn't reach for her, didn't touch her. He just stood there, his gaze holding her prisoner as some unknown emotion flashed in his eyes.

"We didn't use protection."

The words hung in the air—a statement. A question. An accusation. Sammie didn't know what to say, didn't know how to answer. She hadn't given it any thought, had never had to worry about it before, not when they were together. But that had been almost three years ago.

Was he trying to tell her something?

Or was he asking her something?

"I—I'm on birth control."

Jon stepped back, like he'd been slapped. A dozen different emotions flashed in his eyes but it was the last two that took her breath away: anger—and pain.

He turned away, ran a hand through his thick hair, then just stood there with his back to her. His shoulders tensed, the muscles in his broad back bunching as he took a deep breath. A few seconds went by before he turned back to face her.

"Do I need to worry about anything?"

Sammie frowned, not understanding the words—until she did. Her eyes widened in hurt shock and she opened her mouth. Snapped it closed. Opened it again.

"Go to hell."

If he was fazed by her language, he didn't show it. "Don't get all righteous with me, Sammie. It's a valid question. We didn't use protection. So I'll ask again: do I need to worry about anything?"

She wanted to lunge at him. To hit and scream and kick. How could he even ask her that? How could he even *think* it? Sammie didn't bother to answer, just threw a question of her own back at him.

"Do I?"

His eyes never left hers when he answered. "I haven't been with anyone since you, Sammie."

She hadn't expected that answer, didn't want to hear it—even though she knew any other answer would have torn her apart. And how stupid and petty was that? They were no longer married, hadn't been for over two years. It was irrational to think he hadn't—

Except he hadn't, and he wasn't lying—she could see the stark truth in his eyes as he watched her. Unexpected tears suddenly welled in her eyes. She blinked them back, trying to focus instead on the anger still simmering beneath the surface from his silent accusation.

"I haven't been with anyone either." That wasn't exactly what she had planned on telling him. And she hadn't meant to say it so loudly, like it was somehow his fault. "And how dare you even ask me that!"

"You said you were on birth control. What the hell was I supposed to think?"

"That maybe I never stopped taking it. That maybe there are other reasons for it. Like cramps. And heavy periods. And…and—" She stepped closer, leveled an accusing finger at his chest. "And controlling mood swings!"

"Stop raising your voice."

"I am not. Raising. My. Voice." Except she was, because she had seen that stupid flash of male arrogance and satisfaction in his eyes before he managed to blink it away. She wanted to scream at him, tell him that the reason she hadn't been with anyone else was because she was too busy, because her main concern was Clare.

Because she didn't need a man.

She never got to tell him any of that because Clare's voice cut through the thick silence. Small and soft, filled with sleepy confusion—

And just on the other side of the closed door.

"Mommy? Daddy?"

Panic crashed into Sammie. Her gaze darted to the door then shot back to Jon—who was standing there, completely nude.

Just like her.

"Oh God, no. Jon, she can't find us in here together—"

"What are you talking about?"

"Clare. She can't see us like this. Can't know that we...that we—"

Jon closed the small distance between them, his hands closing around her shoulders. "Sammie, stop. It's okay. She's only three. I don't think—"

"Daddy?"

"Jon! You have to do something!" Sammie hissed the words, the panic only marginally held at bay by the sudden urge to hit him. He was laughing! How could he laugh? There was nothing funny about this!

Maybe he saw the murderous urge in her eyes because he stepped back and moved toward the dresser, yanking open two different drawers. He pulled something out of one and tossed it to her, the gray material hitting her in the face.

It was a t-shirt, soft and worn, bearing the insignia

of his old unit on the front. Sammie yanked it over her head, smoothed the hem down as it fell past her thighs. She looked over as Jon stepped into a pair of sweatpants, pulling them up as far as his lean hips. He didn't bother to look at her, didn't even glance over to see if she was dressed, as he reached over and opened the bedroom door.

Clare stepped inside, the bear clutched to her chest, her curls a wild halo around her sleep-creased face. She glanced at Sammie, then turned to Jon, one arm reaching up for him.

"Wanna sleep with you and Mommy."

"Boo, I don't think—"

"You do, huh?"

Clare nodded, her big eyes focused on Jon. He bent over and picked her up, holding her close as he moved toward the bed. He leaned down, readjusted the sheets and comforter with one hand, his gaze never leaving hers.

"Jon, this isn't a good idea."

He settled Clare into the middle of the king size bed then sat down on the edge. "Yeah? Why not?"

"Because—" Because it wasn't. Because it was too much like playing house. Too much like pretending they were a real family.

Because it was too dangerous to her mind. Her heart.

But Sammie couldn't say any of that, not with Clare right there, watching her with sleepy eyes. She wouldn't have been able to say it even if Clare wasn't there, would never admit any of that to Jon.

She shot him one last look then eased onto the bed, shifting on her side and pulling the covers over her and Clare. The mattress dipped as Jon stretched out on the other side, dipped again as he leaned over to turn out the light then rolled toward them.

Sammie lay there for a long time, listening to the sound of Clare's soft breathing. To the sound of Jon's deeper breaths.

And finally fell asleep, letting herself dream, just for tonight, that they were a family again.

chapter
TWENTY-TWO

"Pick it up, ladies! I want to see some speed out there!" Coach Reynolds' voice cut across the ice, the words laced with steely command and what Sammie figured was supposed to be motivation.

She ground her teeth together and pushed harder, her blades digging into the ice. The muscles of her legs stretched, burning as she bent low and hurried across the ice. Faster. Back and forth, sweat pouring from her face, her chest heaving with each breath of cold air she sucked in.

Holy crappola. She hated sprints. Hated them with a passion. They made her feel heavy and slow and out of shape, like she was nothing more than a slug placed on the ice to race a centipede.

Sammie's stride faltered and she nearly fell, gritted her teeth and regained her balance. Where had that crazy comparison even come from? It was stupid, made no sense—further proof that she was losing her mind.

No, not losing her mind. She was just tired. So tired. Work. Practice. Games. Clare. It was getting harder and harder to juggle everything, and she was so afraid that somewhere along the way, she had lost sight of her priorities.

That she was neglecting Clare.

A shrill whistle split the air, signaling an end to the sprints. Sammie slowed to a stop, bent over at the waist, the stick braced across her legs. She sucked in deep gulps of air, willed her heart to slow down.

At least she wasn't the only one who was bent over, sucking in air. Even Taylor and Dani, who were both in much better shape than she was, had sweat rolling down their flushed faces.

Yeah, but they didn't look like they were ready to drop to the ice, gasping like a fish out of water.

It was her own fault, Sammie realized. She hadn't been spending as much time working out as she should have been.

Just one more thing she was trying to juggle, one more ball she was dropping.

Taylor skated over to her, slightly out of breath—which made Sammie feel a little better. "You okay?"

Sammie nodded, finally straightening. She turned her head to the side, wiped her face against her shoulder. "Yeah. Fine."

Taylor studied her for a few seconds then smiled. "If you say so." She placed her stick behind her neck, draped her arms on either side of it, then twisted from side-to-side, stretching. "I hate sprints. God, I hate them so much."

"Glad I'm not the only one." Sammie lowered herself to the ice, braced her hands on her stick, then leaned forward, stretching her back. Her legs. Her entire body.

Telling herself it would be a bad idea—really bad—if she simply just collapsed there and closed her eyes. Only for a minute—

Except she couldn't. They had another hour left in practice before she could shower and go home. Then she had to tuck in Clare—no bedtime story tonight, because her daughter would already be asleep—and go over her lesson plans for the following week. She wouldn't have time to do it this weekend because they had an away game Saturday afternoon then another small demonstration during the first period of the Banners' game Sunday afternoon, followed by an autograph session on the concourse.

She pushed against the stick, rounding her back as she sat back on the heels of her skates, stretching, trying to get rid of this sudden sense of…inadequacy? Failure? Exhaustion?

All of the above.

At least there was one good thing about being so tired, she thought. She hadn't had time to think too much about Jon. About what they'd done two weeks ago.

About what he'd told her.

I never stopped loving you.

Anger swept through her, pushing away some of the exhaustion. What gave him the right to say that? To drop that bomb on her? He didn't have that right, not after what he'd done. Not after the way he'd just abandoned them. It didn't matter that she understood—more than she wanted to. What mattered was that he had made that decision on his own, without giving her a choice. Without giving them a chance.

Sammie jumped to her feet, a burst of anger energizing her as they moved to the next drill, backward snake bites.

Focus. Concentrate. Clear her mind. Knees bent and chest up as she moved through the cones. Fast. Faster.

Except her mind wasn't clear, and she was moving *too* fast, barreling backward into Dani before she could safely stop.

They both fell to the ice, a tangled heap of legs and arms and sticks. Dani rolled to her side, pushed a few strands of her bright copper hair from her face, then jumped to her feet.

"What the hell, Reigs? You know I'm on your team, right?"

"Yeah. Yeah, I'm sorry—" She accepted Dani's hand as the other woman helped her to her feet. "I got carried away."

"You think?" Dani watched her through clear green eyes. Then the woman laughed and clapped a hand on Sammie's shoulder. "As long as you keep that up for Saturday's game, it's all cool."

"Yeah. Cool." Sammie's gaze darted to the boards, where Coach Reynolds was huddled together with Coach Chaney. Had they seen the way she had plowed into Dani? Yeah, probably. They would have had to be blind not to. But they weren't looking this way, didn't seem to be concerned about it.

At least, Coach Reynolds wasn't yelling and screaming and telling her to do laps. That was a bonus.

Coach finally blew the whistle, signaling the end of practice as she waved everyone over. Her gaze swept over them, meeting each player's eyes for a brief second before moving to the next one.

"Thursday's practice is going to be a short one. That doesn't mean we can take it easy. We're playing Philly on Saturday. Out of the three teams, we've had the hardest time against them so far—and it's not because they're better than us."

Coach Reynolds paced in front of them, a clipboard held loosely in one hand, steely determination engraved on her face. "We've outshot them in every game, and we've only managed to beat them once. That stops with Saturday's game. Is that understood?"

"Yes, Coach."

"I'm sorry, what was that? I didn't quite hear you."

"Yes, Coach!"

"One more time."

"Yes, Coach!"

"That's better." The older woman moved back to the center of their group. "Mr. Murphy will be going with us to Saturday's game, along with a few of the other owners."

A low groan echoed around the ice, cut off with an abrupt wave of Coach Reynolds' hand. "I don't want to hear it. He's the owner. His call."

"But he's bad luck."

All eyes turned to Shannon. Her chin shot up in defiance, refusing to back down from the warning look the coaching staff leveled in her direction. Sammie wasn't sure if she should wince in silent sympathy, or applaud the woman for saying what everyone was thinking.

"It's true. Look what happened the last time he went on a road game with us."

"That incident had nothing to with Mr. Murphy's presence." Coach's words lacked their usual command,

and Sammie wondered if she merely felt obligated to say them.

Everyone knew—logically—that Mr. Murphy had nothing to do with Amanda overdosing and being rushed to the hospital. She had done that all on her own. But he'd been there—and it had been the first time he'd ever gone to an away game with them, so of course that meant he was bad luck.

Sammie wasn't sure she really bought into all that superstition stuff, not really. But she didn't exactly want to push the issue, either, figuring it was a case of better safe than sorry.

"That's it for now. Go, get out of here." Coach's eyes darted to Sammie's. "Not you, Reigler."

Unexpected dread filled Sammie and she couldn't shake the feeling that she had just been called to the principal's office. And how ridiculous was that? She wasn't a kid, she hadn't done anything wrong. So why the guilt? Why was Coach singling her out?

Sammie skated over to Coach Reynolds, tried to hide her discomfort and forced herself to stand still, instead of shifting her weight from one foot to the other while Coach Reynolds studied her.

Sammie finally cleared her throat, that feeling of having done something wrong growing stronger with each passing second. "Yes, Coach?"

"You looked a little tired out there tonight. Anything going on you want to talk about?"

Sammie dropped her gaze, not quite able to meet Coach's eyes, and shook her head. "No, Coach. Everything's fine."

"You sure about that? I know you have your hands full, that you're juggling a bit more than anyone else on the team right now."

Was she talking about Jon's sudden reappearance in her life? Because there was no doubt the other woman must know, must have heard—she saw too much *not* to know. Or was she talking about the fact that Sammie was the only parent on the team? Not just a parent—a *single* parent.

Sammie shook her head again, trying to put more confidence in her voice than she felt. "It's all good, Coach. Nothing I can't handle."

"Are you sure?"

"Yes. Absolutely."

"Because if you're not, I need to know."

"I'm sure."

Did Coach Reynolds hear the tiny hint of doubt in Sammie's voice? Had she noticed the way Sammie couldn't quite meet her gaze for more than a second at a time? Probably. But she didn't say anything about it, didn't call Sammie out on it, just simply nodded.

"Okay, I'll take you at your word for now. But if anything changes, I need to know."

"Yes, Coach." Sammie turned, started to skate away when Coach called out to her.

"Reigler—if you need to talk, we're here."

Sammie nodded again and turned away, swallowing against the lump in her throat and the tightness in her chest. *We*, the coach had said.

Maybe the other woman really meant it, or maybe it was nothing more than a turn of phrase, meant to reassure Sammie.

It didn't matter because it did the trick—the words *were* reassuring, reminding her again that she was part of something bigger now.

That she wasn't as alone as she sometimes felt.

chapter
TWENTY-THREE

Jonathan stood in the entranceway of the Victorian farmhouse, hands shoved into the front pockets of his jeans as he waited, feeling every inch the outsider.

He hadn't been invited inside, hadn't been told to have a seat or make himself comfortable while he waited. He was surprised he'd been allowed in this far, that Mr. Warner hadn't forced him to wait outside on the porch, in the bitter cold.

In fact, he was surprised that Sammie's dad had let him inside at all, that he hadn't slammed the door in Jonathan's face. Yeah, probably because Sammie's mom had been standing there—she'd placed a hand on her husband's arm and stepped around him, telling Jonathan to come inside—

And to wait right there while Sammie went to get Clare ready.

Fair enough, Jonathan thought. He didn't blame them for the cold welcome, for the barely-concealed anger and confusion in their eyes as they looked him over. If the positions were reversed, he'd feel the same way: cautious, protective, angry. Bitter. Doubtful. Hell, he'd divorced their daughter, turned his back on their granddaughter. Nothing could excuse that.

He didn't think telling them he agreed with them would help anything so he just stood there, waiting.

Trying to ignore the harsh whispers coming from the kitchen at the back of the house. It was becoming harder and harder to do because the angry words weren't really being whispered anymore—

And because they were about him.

He should have given this more thought, should have realized coming here had been a bad idea. It was early Saturday morning, the sun barely peeking over the horizon, and he was here to pick up Clare before Sammie had to hit the road for her game in Philly this afternoon. She had offered to drop Clare off at his place—grudgingly, because it was obvious she didn't even want Clare to spend the day with him—but he talked her out of it. Had told Sammie it would be easier for him to pick Clare up, so she wouldn't have to rush around, so she would have one less thing to worry about. Jonathan had honestly thought he was being helpful. He could see the exhaustion in Sammie's eyes, could feel the tension rolling off her in waves every single time he saw her.

Just like he saw the worry and doubt clinging to her. And he knew—absolutely knew, with crystal clear certainty—that she was doubting herself, telling herself that she was doing too much. Worrying that she was neglecting Clare. She hadn't said anything to make him think that, but he still knew, could see it in her eyes.

And he could hear it in the underlying tones of the angry voices coming from the kitchen.

"She shouldn't be going anywhere with him, Samantha."

"He's her father."

"Which means nothing. That doesn't give him any rights, not when he hasn't been here for her at all."

A long pause, broken by a weary sigh. Sammie's voice.

Tired, drained. "He's trying, Dad."

"Too damn late, if you ask me."

"Dennis, keep your voice down."

"Why? Let him hear." The sound of heavy footsteps, moving across the tile floor. "After everything he did to our daughter? Our granddaughter? I can't believe you're okay with this, Margaret."

"It's not up to me, Dennis. And it's not up to you. This is between Sammie and Jonathan."

"Not as far as I'm concerned, it isn't."

"Dad, please. You're not helping."

"Not helping? And you think you are? Do you really think letting Clare spend time with that man is good for her?"

"Dad—"

"It's not. Maybe if you spent more time at home, with your daughter, instead of running around, you could see that."

Jonathan heard a sharp gasp, knew the sound came from Sammie's mother. He held his breath, waiting for Sammie to say something, to argue or tell her father he was wrong or—something. What he heard instead made his blood freeze.

"Maybe you're right. Maybe I should just quit hockey."

Jonathan moved from his spot by the door. He wanted to storm along the hallway, wanted to race into to the kitchen and jump to Sammie's defense. But he didn't, not yet. He kept his steps silent, his moves slow and deliberate as he made his way toward the back of the house, listening as the shocked silence that greeted Sammie's words slowly faded.

Her mother spoke first, her voice low and urgent. "Sammie, no. You don't mean that. After you worked so hard—"

"If she wants to quit, Margaret, let her. She needs to focus on her priorities."

"How can you even say that, Dennis?" Mrs. Warner's

voice grew a little louder, the words holding more than a hint of anger. "After all the encouragement you gave her? After telling her how much you believed in her?"

"I do believe in her. But it's too much. Even you can see that, see how tired she is all the time, how drained she is. Something has to go. Hockey is the only thing that makes sense—"

"Sammie's not quitting." Jonathan's quiet words pierced the tension blanketing the room. He stood in the doorway, not moving, not even flinching as three sets of eyes stared at him.

Dennis Warner took a step toward him, his face a hard mask of warning. "This doesn't concern you, Reigler."

Jonathan ignored him, his gaze focused on Sammie—and only on her. Her face was pale, her dark eyes looking even larger because of the smudged circles under them. He could see the exhaustion clinging to her, saw the way her eyes filled with indecision and uncertainty.

"Jon, please, not now—"

"You can't quit, Sammie. You don't *need* to quit."

"I can't—" She stopped, chewed on her lower lip as her gaze darted from him to her parents. "I'll go get Clare."

She brushed past him, hurrying from the room. Jonathan turned, watched her disappear around the corner, heard the echo of her footsteps as she ran upstairs. He turned back, tension tightening his shoulders as her parents stared at him.

Then her mother brushed past him as well, briefly reaching for his arm and squeezing as she muttered something about helping Sammie. Jonathan had no idea what to make of that touch, didn't know if she was encouraging him, sympathizing with him…or warning him.

Mr. Warner crossed his arms in front of his wide chest, a scowl lining his weathered face. "You shouldn't be here, Reigler."

"I'm just here to pick up Clare."

"That's not what I'm talking about." The older man

stepped closer, his gaze boring into Jonathan's. "You should have never come back. You should have stayed away."

"That wasn't an option, sir."

"There are always options."

"Not always." Jonathan met the man's steely gaze head-on, refusing to look away. Silently letting the older man know he wasn't going anywhere, that he wasn't leaving. He wasn't walking away. Not this time.

Not from this. Not from Clare.

Not from Sammie.

"You being here—" The older man shook his head, an expression of worry creasing his face. "It's not good. Not for either of them."

"Clare's my daughter. I'm not leaving her again."

"Even if Sammie has to pay the price?"

"The price? What price? Sammie isn't—"

"She still loves you, you know. She won't admit it, but she does." Mr. Warner forced the words between clenched teeth, as if he was reporting the world had just come to an end.

Jonathan ignored the way his heart slammed into his chest, ignored the way that tiny little spark of hope he'd been holding close grew into a small flame. He released a quick breath, his gaze never wavering. "That doesn't concern—"

"Don't you dare tell me it doesn't concern me. I'm her father. Everything about her concerns me, no matter how old she gets." The older man stepped forward, pointed one thick finger at Jonathan's chest. "You being here only complicates things. She's spreading herself too thin, spending too much time worrying about *you*. Everything was fine before you showed back up. You see how tired she is now. She's doing too much, dealing with too much—"

"So telling her she should give up hockey solves everything?"

"If it forces her to realize she's spending too much time worrying about you? Forces her to see that things were better before you came back? Then absolutely."

"That's not up to you, Dennis."

"Don't stand there and tell me it's not up to me. I think I know what's best for my daughter."

"Is that what you think? Really? You think this is going to help?" Jonathan ignored the finger poking him in the chest. He stepped closer, his voice dangerously low. "It won't. It will be the worst thing you've ever done. Don't make the mistake of thinking you know what's best for Sammie, of not giving her a choice. I made that same mistake and I'll regret it for the rest of my life."

Shock spread across the older man's face. Jonathan ignored it. Ignored the way the man's eyes widened in his lined face, ignored the truth that slowly dawned in their depths. He spun around, hurried from the kitchen—and nearly knocked Sammie over as she rounded the corner by the stairs. He caught himself at the last minute, stepped back and gulped in a deep breath of air as Clare looked up at him and smiled.

He reached for her, his hands brushing against Sammie's. It was the first time they had touched since the night they had spent together. Did Sammie feel the same jolt? Or was the blush staining her cheeks caused by something else?

He settled Clare in his arms, reached out and took both bags from Sammie, his hand lingering on hers. She pulled away, the blush deepening even more.

"You'll have her back before bedtime?"

"Yes."

"And you'll make sure—"

"Sammie, she'll be fine. Stop worrying. You need to get ready to leave for your game."

"I—" Her mouth closed, shutting off whatever she'd been about to say. Jonathan saw the sorrow that filled her eyes, felt her hesitation and doubt.

He tossed the bags over his shoulder, freeing one hand, then reached out and tucked a loose curl behind Sammie's ear. "Don't quit, Sammie."

"It's not that easy. You don't understand—"

"Yes, I do."

"You don't. You don't know what it's like, trying to juggle everything, always worrying. Work. Practice. Being a single parent—"

"But you're not. Not anymore."

Her eyes widened for a split-second. Her gaze shifted to his hand, where it still rested on her shoulder, his thumb rubbing slow circles along the base of her neck. She shook her head, stepped back with a look of determination—and sorrow.

"I can't count on that, Jon."

The words sliced deep, hurting more than he could imagine. He ignored the pain, pushed it away. "You can."

"How? How do I know that? You walked away once, Jon. How can I trust you not to do the same thing again?"

"Because I won't."

"I don't know that."

"Then I'll prove it to you."

"I don't think—"

Jonathan dipped his head, cut her off with a gentle brush of his lips against hers. He heard her swift intake of breath, felt her body lean closer—

Before she stiffened and pulled away.

"We can talk later. You need to get ready for your game."

"Jon—"

"Don't do anything you're going to regret, okay? We can talk later. Just—go out and give them hell this afternoon." He stepped away, turned to face Clare and gave her a little bounce. "Isn't that right, Little Bits? Tell Mommy to go kick some butt."

Clare giggled, bouncing up and down as she clapped her hands. "Mommy. Go kick butt. Now."

"Jon! That's not even funny!" But laughter chased away some of the shadows lurking in Sammie's eyes, and Jonathan could see she was fighting not to smile.

"Uh-oh, Little Bits. I think Daddy's in trouble."

Sammie raised her brows, the smile she had been fighting finally breaking free, gently curling one corner of her mouth. "Gee, you think?"

"It was worth it." He cupped her cheek, ran his thumb across her lower lip, then dropped his hand and stepped back. "Okay, Little Bits. Time to let Mommy get ready for her game. Give her a kiss and tell her good luck."

Clare giggled and did just that, adding a high-five for good measure. Jonathan opened the door and stepped outside, then stopped and turned back to Sammie.

"No decisions, Sammie, okay? Not until we talk?"

He waited, breathing a sigh of relief when she finally nodded. It wasn't much, but he'd take it.

For now.

chapter
TWENTY-FOUR

"You're not quitting."

"I didn't say I *was*. I said I was thinking about it."

"Fucking semantics. You're not even thinking about it. Not allowed."

"You can't tell me what I can and can't think. It doesn't work that way."

Shannon leaned closer, forcing Sammie to step back. She collided with the wall then shot a desperate look at Taylor, silently asking for help. Only no help would be coming from that direction, she knew that with just one glance. Taylor looked stunned, and almost as furious as Shannon.

"Guys, come one. You're supposed to be my friends. You're supposed to support me."

"Not when you start talking stupid shit like this, we're not. I mean, what the fuck, Reigs? Where is this even coming from?"

"I told you, it's getting to be too much. And I only

said I was thinking about it."

Shannon threw her hands in the air, then brought them straight down on top of her head. She closed her eyes and made a low sound in the back of her throat that came out like a growl. Sammie stepped to the side, actually worried that Shannon was ready to come undone.

Taylor caught her arm, holding her in place and pinning her with a confused look. "But why? I don't get it."

"There's nothing to get. I'm just—I don't know if I can do this anymore."

"But *why*?"

"Because I'm tired."

"We're all tired, Sammie. You don't see anyone else saying they're going to quit." Taylor pointed behind her, but the gesture was empty—they were the only three in the room.

Sammie should have never said anything. She wasn't even sure why she had. But she'd been thinking about it during the entire bus ride up to Philly, and instead of coming to any conclusions, she was more confused than ever. So she'd gotten dressed then dragged Taylor and Shannon to the small bathroom, needing to talk to someone.

That had been a mistake, because both women looked like they were ready to lose it, torn between confusion and anger and worry.

"I should have never said anything—"

"But you did. You can't just drop something like that on us and walk away." Taylor released her hold on Sammie's arm then started pacing around the small room. "What happened? Why this change of heart all of a sudden?"

"It's not a change of heart. I don't *want* to quit. I just don't—"

"Fuck, Reigs. Out with it already. You're totally fucking with my mojo."

"What? How can I mess with your mojo—"

"OhmyGod, will you just answer the question already! What's going on? Where's this coming from?"

Sammie's gaze slid from Shannon to Taylor. "I told you, I'm tired."

"Yeah? And?"

"And...I don't know if I can keep this schedule up."

"What schedule? Practices? Games? That's only three days a week."

"Yeah. And then there's work. I have a full-time job, remember? And I'm a mom. I have to think about Clare."

"I thought part of the reason you were doing this was for Clare."

"I was. I am."

"Then what's the issue? What's really going on?"

Shannon leaned closer, her brows lowered in a scary frown. "Does this have something to do with your ex? Is that what this is about? Because I have no problem kicking his fucking ass."

"What? No. Jon wants me to keep playing." At least, Sammie thought he did, if his reaction this morning meant anything.

"Then what, exactly, is the issue? Because all of us work."

"Which totally fucking sucks, because you know if we were a men's team, we wouldn't—"

"Shannon! Not now!" Taylor turned back to Sammie. "Out with it. What else is going on?"

Sammie opened her mouth, closed it with a snap. How could she explain, when she didn't understand herself? It wasn't just because she was tired, she knew that much. And it wasn't just because she was worried about not spending enough time with Clare, although that played a huge part in her fears.

She dropped her gaze to the floor, unable to meet the gaze of the other women. "I'm not sure. I mean, I *am* tired. And yes, I know we all are. I know I'm not the only one with a full-time job. But I need to worry about Clare, too. What if I'm not spending enough time with her? Especially now that Jon's in the picture and spending so much time with her."

The words echoed off the cracked tile of the dirty floors and walls, bouncing around them. Sammie kept staring at the floor, waiting for the other two women to say something. To sympathize. To give her words of encouragement. To commiserate.

Something.

All she heard was silence.

Sammie finally lifted her head then jerked back in surprise, hitting her elbow against the edge of the sink. Shannon and Taylor were staring at her, but not in sympathy.

Not even close.

"You're jealous."

"What? I am *not*."

"You are, too. You're fucking jealous."

"I think Shannon's right."

"No. No way." Sammie shook her head so fast, her vision spun. She stopped, blinked, waited for her vision to clear, then denied it again. "No. I am not jealous. There's nothing to be jealous of."

"That's exactly what you are. You don't want to

share Clare with him."

"Don't be ridiculous." No. They were both crazy. This had nothing to do with Jon.

Did it?

No, it didn't. It *couldn't*.

Could it? Was she really that petty?

"I think it does. I mean, this wasn't even an issue until a few weeks ago. Isn't that when he started spending time with Clare?"

"Yeah, maybe. But that doesn't mean—"

"That's exactly what it means. Face it, Reigs. You're used to having Clare all to yourself. You don't want to share her."

"*Share* her? Shannon, she's my daughter. Not some kind of toy. And—"

"Whatever." Shannon waved a hand, brushing her off. "You get my point. And it's stupid."

"How can you say it's stupid? She's my *daughter*!"

"It's not *stupid*." Taylor shot a meaningful glance at Shannon then turned back to Sammie. "But Shannon has a point. You're not used to having anyone else in Clare's life."

"That doesn't mean anything." And it didn't. It absolutely didn't mean anything.

Except she was afraid it did. And oh God, what kind of mean, smallminded person did that make her?

"It's not a big deal."

"Shannon—"

"And I have the perfect solution." Shannon talked right over Sammie, ignoring her objections and Taylor's wild gesturing. "Just move in with him."

Startled silence settled over the small room—not just from Sammie, but from Taylor, too. But Taylor recovered quicker than Sammie.

"Are you out of your freaking mind?"

"No. Why would you say that?"

"Because he's her *ex-husband*, that's why! On what planet does that even make sense?"

Shannon brushed Taylor's objections off then turned to Sammie. "You're sleeping with him, right?"

"I—no." Sammie stopped shaking her head when Shannon shot her a disbelieving glare. "One time. That was it. It didn't mean anything."

"OhmyGod, Sammie! Why didn't you say something?"

"Really? It didn't mean anything?"

Sammie looked back and forth between her two teammates, trying to figure out who to answer first. Shannon was the bigger threat. "No, it didn't. It just…kind of happened."

"Uh-huh. And how many other men have you been with in the last two years?"

"That doesn't—"

"How many?"

Sammie narrowed her eyes, thought about not answering…and realized that wasn't an option, not with the way Shannon was staring at her. "None."

"Yet you slept with your ex. What does that tell you?"

"Nothing. And what does any of this have to do with what we were talking about?"

"Everything, that's what. You think you're missing out on spending time with Clare because she's spending time with your ex. You're already sleeping with him—"

"It was *one time*—"

"So just move in with him. Problem solved."

"Why would I move in with him?"

"Because you still love him. Duh."

Sammie stared at Shannon in open-mouth shock, her mind completely blank. She had no idea what to say, how to respond. That was—

"That is the most ridiculous thing I have ever heard. Where did that come from? I mean, seriously. How does that mind of yours even work?"

"Oh please. You know it's true. Look at her!" Shannon waved a hand in Sammie's direction. "She still loves him. You know it. I know it. And she knows it, too—she just hasn't admitted it to herself yet."

"I can't." Sammie's denial fell from lips that felt oddly numb. "I don't even trust him!"

"Let me ask you something." Shannon's voice softened, understanding and insight flashing in her eyes. "Where's Clare now?"

"With Jon. But that doesn't mean—"

"You wouldn't leave her with someone you don't trust."

"That's not the same thing—"

"Yeah, keep telling yourself that. I know better. And so do you." Shannon tapped her on the head the three times with her knuckles. "Now I have to go do extra work on my mojo, try to get it back after this little interruption."

Sammie opened her mouth—to disagree, to complain about being knuckled, to say something about Shannon's mojo. She never got the chance because the door swung open and Coach Reynolds stormed in, pinning all three of them in place with her furious gaze.

"Is there something going on in here I need to know about?"

"No, Coach."

"Then is there a reason the three of you are in here, instead of out on the ice, warming up?"

"No—"

"Reigs was talking about quitting."

"Shannon!" Taylor hissed her name, shot an apologetic look at Sammie. "Coach, it's not—"

"Wiley and LeBlanc. Out. Now."

Shannon and Taylor hesitated, glanced at Sammie, then hurried from the room. Coach Reynolds moved in front of the door, her dark eyes studying Sammie. Judging. Weighing. Sammie shifted under the scrutiny, forced herself not to look away.

"You quitting, Reigler?"

Was she?

The answer came to her immediately. No, she wasn't quitting. Taylor was right, she had worked too hard for this. All of them had. She didn't *want* to quit. And quitting wouldn't help with the real issue, now that Shannon had—in typical Shannon-fashion—tossed the real issue straight into Sammie's face.

She straightened, shook her head. "No, Coach."

"Then get your ass out to the ice where you belong. Now."

"Yes, Coach."

Chapter TWENTY-FIVE

"You know we only won yesterday because I was able to fix my mojo."

Sammie snorted her disbelief. "Yeah, okay."

"No, seriously. It is."

"If you say so."

"Of course I say so. It had nothing to do with your fucking goal."

"Shannon! Watch your language?"

"What? It's not like there's anyone here." She waved her hand, the motion taking in the empty concourse where they were set up to sign autographs. The Blades had done their ten-minute scrimmage during the Banners' first intermission, then come out here for the meet-and-greet afterward. Four tables had been set-up in different sections, and Sammie was sitting with Shannon, Dani, and Taylor.

But the game had started again, and the small

crowd that had come out to see them had disappeared—along with Taylor, who had made some excuse about getting something to drink. That had been almost fifteen minutes ago, and she still wasn't back.

And the concourse wasn't completely empty— a few fans were walking around, their hands filled with trays weighed down with soda and beer and nachos. But for the most part, they had the concourse to themselves. Fans were either in the stands, cheering for the Banners as they played against Vegas, or sitting at home, watching the game on television because of the weather.

Sammie glanced out the large window to her left, frowning at the snow falling and blowing and covering the sidewalks and street. The forecasters had been calling for a light dusting, but they had surpassed that over an hour ago. Sammie hoped it stopped, soon, before they left, because she hated driving in the snow.

"So yeah, us winning yesterday had nothing to do with your goal." Shannon kept talking as she doodled on a flyer advertising the Blades' upcoming games. "Even if it was abso-fucking-lutely beautiful."

Sammie slid down in the metal chair and fiddled with the marker in her hand. "It was pure dumb luck, and you know it."

And it had been. Sammie had been covering one of Philly's players, sticking to her like glue to prevent a pass. The player who had possession of the puck either didn't see Sammie, or had decided to pass it anyway. Or maybe it had been nothing more than a mistake. It didn't matter, because the puck had landed against Sammie's tape with beautiful precision, just begging her to take control.

After a split-second of hesitation—because she couldn't believe what just happened—she finally spun around and took off, never looking back, bracing herself for a hit or a trip or something. And then she was there, in front of the net, just her and Philly's goalie. She almost took the straight shot, had actually pulled back with her stick. But she saw their goalie move at the last second to block it, watched in disbelief as the woman slid out of position. Sammie shifted right, moved closer, and buried the puck into the back of the net.

Her first goal of the season.

It didn't register at first, even as she stood there, watching the red light flash above the net. It wasn't until Taylor and Dani and Sydney and Rachel had come up to her, slapping her on the back and tapping her on the head, that she finally realized what she'd done.

She had scored!

And it wasn't just her first goal of the season—it had been the game-winning goal, too.

"Dumb luck or not, it was still a beautiful shot. And the look on your face. That was priceless." Dani shook her head, laughing. "We really need to see if we can get a still from the video and have it printed."

Sammie cringed. They had watched some of the video saved from the live stream on the bus ride back home. The angle had been from directly behind the net and showed her standing there, the mouthpiece dangling from her open mouth and the stick dangling from her loose fingers. She had looked totally and completely stunned—and not in a good way. "No, we don't. Really."

"But it's a beautiful shot!"

"Holy crappola, it is not! I looked stupid."

"Not stupid. Stupefied, maybe, but not stupid."

"Oooo, good one, Baldwin." Shannon nudged Dani in the side, snorting. Sammie rolled her eyes, ready to tell them both they were crazy, but a small family approached the table—a mom and dad and two kids, obviously brother and sister. The girl, maybe six or seven years old, bounced up to Shannon with a wide smile that showed a gap from a missing tooth. She held a Blades jersey with Shannon's last name screen-printed across the back.

"I'm going to be a goalie, too!"

Sammie bit the inside of her cheek to keep from laughing at the shocked expression that crossed Shannon's face. The woman was stunned speechless, her mouth hanging slightly ajar. Dani smothered her own laugh and pushed away from the table, easing behind the family and snapping a picture with her phone.

Shannon blinked, recovering enough to shoot Dani a warning glance, then leaned across the table toward the little girl. "That's awesome because goalies totally rock."

"I know!" The girl bounced up and down, looked over her shoulder, then pushed the jersey across the table toward Shannon with a shy look. "I want to be just like you when I grow up. That's why I have your jersey. Can you sign it for me please?"

The hero worship on the little girl's face made Sammie's heart melt. And hers wasn't the only one. Dani clapped a hand over her mouth, smothering her whispered "Aww."

But it was Shannon who surprised her the most. The normally tough-as-nails, mouthy, opinionated woman sat there with tears in her eyes, looking like she was ready to turn into a puddle of gooey emotion. Sammie blinked, wondering if she was simply imagining it. No, she wasn't. Shannon was totally floored by the little girl staring up at her with hero-worship in her eyes, waiting for her to sign the jersey.

And waiting some more…

Sammie kicked Shannon under the table, swallowing another laugh when she jerked back in surprise. Shannon blinked, shook her head, then reached for the jersey.

"That's awesome. Of course, I'll sign it." Shannon smoothed the jersey on the table in front of her and reached for a marker, then signed her name with a flourish, a big grin on her face the entire time. The little girl jumped up and down again then tugged the jersey over her head.

"Can I get my picture, too?"

"Absolutely!" Shannon's grin grew even wider as she pushed away from the table then stood next to the little girl, bending down and draping her arm over her thin shoulders.

"Oh hey, hang on a second." Shannon moved toward her gear bag behind the table, reached down and grabbed her stick. "Every goalie needs a good stick, right?"

The girl's mouth dropped open, the hero-worship growing brighter in her eyes as she reached for the stick that was at least twice her size. Shannon grabbed the marker, signed her name on the blade, then posed for another picture.

The girl's younger brother, obviously annoyed at being left out for so long, made a loud huffing sound and crossed his thin arms in front of him. "That's just stupid. Girls can't be goalies. They can't even play hockey."

The parents gasped, the mother reaching for the little boy as she tried to apologize. Shannon's eyes narrowed as she leaned down, no doubt ready to open her mouth and let loose with a verbal tirade she wouldn't be able to take back. Sammie thought about vaulting over the table to stop her but there was no way she'd be able to move that fast. And Dani was too far away—

"I wouldn't be so sure of that. Have you ever seen these ladies play? Because I have, and I wouldn't mind having them on my team." The deep voice drifted over the small crowd, leaving stunned silence in its wake. Sammie looked over, staring at the newcomer in surprise.

Tall, with dark hair and piercing green eyes and a crooked smile that hinted at a dimple in his right cheek. An expensive black suit draped his body, tailored to fit broad shoulders and lean waist and strong, muscular legs. One of his legs was bent at the knee, his foot encased in a soft cast. The man's hands curled around the handles of the two crutches braced under his arms, supporting him.

The little boy's eyes widened as he stared at the newcomer, obviously stunned speechless. And he wasn't the only one. Shannon stood there as well, still slightly bent over, her mouth still open on whatever she'd been about to tell the young boy.

Shannon quickly straightened, tugged on her jersey, ran a hand through her long blonde hair.

And holy crappola, she was blushing! Shannon was actually blushing!

The man introduced himself—yeah, right, because nobody knew who Caleb Johnson, one of the

Banners' star players, was—then posed for pictures with both the little boy and the family before they left. Shannon stood there for a second, looking completely flustered, then raced around the table and dropped into her chair.

And yes, she was still blushing. Unbelievable.

Caleb stepped closer to the table, nodded at Sammie and Dani, then leaned toward Shannon. Or maybe it was just the way he was resting on his crutches that made it look that way. "Classy move, giving her your stick."

"Oh. Um, well." Shannon cleared her throat, fidgeted with the marker in her hand, looked around at everything except the man in front of her. "Yeah. I guess. Thanks."

Dani started laughing, clapped a hand over her mouth as the laughter turned into a coughing fit. Sammie dug her nails into her palms and looked away, afraid she'd start laughing, too. This was a side of Shannon she had never seen, had never even guessed at. How could anyone have ever guessed that Shannon—of all people—was even capable of being flustered?

Sammie looked over again, just to make sure she really wasn't seeing things, then blinked in surprise when her gaze landed on two people walking toward them.

Taylor, carrying a cardboard tray filled with cups of soda, and…

Jon.

Sammie straightened in her chair, wondering if she was hallucinating. No, that was really Jon. Their eyes met, and her heart did a quick tumble-roll when his lips turned up in a smile.

She started to stand, then dropped back into the seat. What was she doing? Had she really been ready to go over to him and...and what? Put her arms around him? Kiss him?

No. No, of course not. That was ridiculous. The reaction had been nothing more than a stupid impulse, a result of yesterday's conversation with Shannon and Taylor before *and* after the game—because they hadn't dropped it. Or maybe she was simply being hit with the residual hormones bouncing off Shannon as she kept squirming in her chair, staring up at Caleb Johnson.

Taylor put the tray of drinks on the table and started passing around cups, her gaze meeting Sammie's for a few long seconds before she tilted her head in Jon's direction. "Guess who I found wandering around the concourse?"

"Uh, yeah, I see that." Sammie cleared her throat, doing a little squirming of her own. "Jon. What are you doing here?"

"Mac's never been to a hockey game before so I figured I'd bring him."

"Mac?" Sammie glanced around, searching for Jon's friend.

"He's still watching the game."

"Oh." Sammie cleared her throat again, wondering what else to say, wondering why Jon was watching her like that, with his mouth curled into a smile and a glimmer of heat and amusement dancing in his eyes.

A sudden suspicion formed in her mind and she turned to Taylor, frowning, wondering what her friend had been up to. She was ready to ask, but Taylor pasted a bright smile on her face and started talking.

"Caleb, you didn't tell them, did you?"

The hockey player shook his head. "No. You

swore me to secrecy, Tay-Tay. I know better."

"Tell us what?"

"Yeah, *Tay-Tay*," Sammie put as much menace in her name as possible. "Tell us what?"

"I was going to wait until later to surprise you—"

"Really?"

Taylor narrowed her eyes at Sammie, then kept talking. "The exhibition game is a go!"

"Are you serious?"

"For real?"

Taylor nodded, a wide grin on her face. "Seriously for real. Chuckie just finalized all the details."

The stunned silence lasted for three seconds, then they all jumped up and down, laughing and hugging each other.

"He did it! He really did it!"

"Holy crappola. I can't believe it! It's really happening."

"I told you he would. When will you guys start believing me?"

"I know but—I mean, wow."

Jon looked around, amusement warring with confusion. "So what's happening?"

Dani answered him before Sammie could. "An exhibition game. With the Banners. A *real* game."

"Yeah. One *you* would have missed if you had quit yesterday."

"I wasn't—"

"Wait. Hang on." Jon stepped closer to her, a frown creasing his face. "You said you weren't going to do anything until we talked."

"I didn't. I wasn't." Sammie rested her hand against his chest, surprised to feel the steady pounding of his heart beating against her palm. "I'm not. It was just—I'll explain later, okay?"

Jon watched her, his dark gaze seeing too much—and showing too much. Worry. Concern. Pride. And...

Sammie swallowed and tried to look away, tried to step back. He reached for her hand, threaded his fingers with hers, and squeezed. "Later."

The promise in his eyes scared her. No, not scared. That was the wrong word. Yes, she was scared, but not because of Jon. Not because of the way he was looking at her, of what she saw in his deep gaze. She was scared of what she felt, the way her body tightened and warmed. The way she wanted to lean against him, the way her stomach dipped and swirled simply because he was holding her hand.

She glanced over at her teammates, wondering if they could see it, but none of them were looking at her. They were still talking about the exhibition game, excitement and surprise clear in their voices and on their faces.

Except for Shannon, who was still blushing as she slid flirty little glances in Caleb's direction.

The excitement finally died down, the conversation turning to the weather. Caleb said goodbye to everyone, his gaze lingering on Shannon as he turned to leave. Taylor waited a few seconds then grabbed Shannon by the arm and shook her.

"Don't even think about it."

"What? I'm not thinking about anything."

"Oh yes, you are. I can see it on your face. Do *not* go there."

"What are you talking about?"

"She's talking about the way the temperature shot up to a hundred-and-fifty from all that lust rolling off of you." Amusement danced in Dani's green eyes as she waved a hand in front of her face. "Whew. I thought you were going to jump him right here."

"I was not!" But Shannon's face turned bright red and she looked away.

"Um, maybe I should go back inside—"

"No, you're good. We're all done here anyway." Taylor waved Jon's objections off then turned back to Shannon. "And I mean it. Don't go there. Caleb is a nice guy but he is, like, the biggest player ever. The. *Biggest*. So just don't."

"I wasn't—"

"Were too. Just trust me on this. For once."

"But—"

"For once. Please."

Shannon threw her hands up in the air and let out a little growl. "Fine. Whatever. But I'd like to point out that I'm not the one standing here with moon eyes, holding her ex-husband's hand!"

All three of her teammates turned, glanced down at Jon's hand wrapped around hers, then looked back at Sammie—grinning.

Heat filled her face and she almost yanked her hand from Jon's, especially when he started chuckling. Instead, she tilted her chin up and shot all three women a warning scowl.

"You're just jealous." Then she tugged Jon's hand and started walking in the other direction, away from the laughter and catcalls.

chapter
TWENTY-SIX

Sammie gazed out the passenger window, staring at the swirling snow as it fell around them, coating the trees. The streets. The windshield.

She curled her hands together in her lap and closed her eyes, listening as the wipers slid across the cold glass. *Thwamp-thwamp-thwamp.* Fast. Back and forth, over and over, working hard to keep up with the driving snow.

Sammie was grateful that she wasn't driving. Jon must have seen her staring out the windows of the concourse, must have seen the worry on her face as she studied the heavy snow. He had squeezed her hand and offered to drive her home.

She didn't accept at first, afraid of sounding too eager, using the excuse that he had to get his own vehicle back home. But he'd told her that he didn't have his car, that Mac had picked him up in his big truck.

That it would be no problem for him to drive her home.

Sammie didn't bother searching for more excuses after that and finally accepted his offer. Maybe she shouldn't have, maybe it wasn't a smart thing to do, but she hated driving in this kind of weather. Hated it, always had, ever since she was seventeen and had spun out on an icy road, nearly taking out a tree before sliding to a stop against a mailbox.

Of course, the downside to letting Jon drive was being trapped in the small confines of her car with him. Not that she felt trapped—which was the problem.

She snuck a glance at him from the corner of her eye, studying his strong profile. The slight ridge of his nose. The shadow of stubble shading his jaw. Hard. Competent. A witness to horrors she couldn't even imagine. There was an inner strength there—but vulnerability, too. She could see it in the shadows that occasionally crossed his face. In the surprise that danced in his eyes when he watched Clare, like he couldn't believe she was there, couldn't believe she was his.

And she could see it in the heat in his eyes when he occasionally looked at her. He was so careful to hide it—usually. But there had been a few times when she'd glimpsed it, before he could blink it away.

All she could see now was competence, in the way one powerful hand gripped the steering wheel as he maneuvered the car up the interstate. Strong. Relaxed. In charge.

She trusted him.

The realization should surprise her but it didn't. After everything they'd been through, after the pain she had carried for more than two years, she shouldn't trust him. There was no logical reason for it. But she did.

Shannon had been right. Whether he was Clare's father or not, Sammie would have never left her with Jon if she didn't trust him.

But what about everything else? The way her heart skipped and danced whenever he was near. The way her stomach fluttered when he smiled at her. The way her palms grew warm and itched to touch him, even now.

That had nothing to do with trust.

Or maybe it had everything to do with it.

"Are you going to tell me what I missed back there?"

"Hm?" Sammie turned her head, felt her face heat when she realized where her thoughts had been heading. "Miss what?"

Jon chuckled, the sound making the heat from her face spread lower. "That's what I asked. Back at the arena. Why do I feel like I missed something?"

"Oh, that. You didn't. That was just Shannon and Taylor being themselves. Thinking they were being funny."

"Why am I not buying that?"

Sammie shrugged and shifted in the seat, slid her gaze out the window.

"Okay then, how about what else they said? About you quitting. What was that all about?"

"Nothing."

Jon was quiet for a long minute, long enough that Sammie started to think he was letting the subject drop. He did, only to replace it with another one she didn't want to think about.

He reached over and grabbed her hand, curled his fingers around it then gently raised it between them.

His voice was as soft as his eyes when he spoke. "Then what about this? What was that all about? Because you've gone out of your way to *not* touch me since the night we spent together."

Sammie tensed, her mind searching for an answer—any answer—to give him. But her mind was dangerously blank. She looked away, ready to pull her hand from his. The car started sliding, back and forth, veering across both lanes of 83. Fear knotted her stomach. Her fingers tightened around his, even though she knew she needed to let go of his hand, that he needed both hands to take control of the car—

But he guided the car out of the slide with ease, expertly maneuvering it back into the right lane. He glanced down at their clasped hands, at the way her fingers gripped his own so tight, the flesh of her knuckles turned white.

Jon squeezed her hand then raised it to his mouth and pressed a quick kiss to her fingers. "Just a little slide, not a big deal."

"I—I know." And she needed to pull her hand from his, she really needed to.

"You still hate driving in this stuff, huh?"

"Um, yeah. I guess I do."

"Well, no need to worry. I'll have you home in no time. Safe and sound."

"Then what about you? How are you going to get home?"

"Mac's going to pick me up."

Sammie glanced out the window, at the falling snow that seemed to grow heavier with each passing minute. "It looks like it's getting worse."

"It's not too bad."

"You, uh, you could always stay with us, instead

of having Mac drive all the way out to pick you up. There's plenty of room—"

"Somehow I don't think your parents would appreciate that too much."

"They wouldn't mind." Jon glanced over, one brow raised in disbelief. Sammie shrugged and looked away. "Okay, maybe they would. But they'd get over it."

"I think I'll just have Mac pick me up."

"But I feel bad—"

"It's not a big deal, Sammie. Honest."

"I think you should just go to your place. It's closer."

"And then what? You're going to drive home? Sammie, no. You hate driving in this stuff. Mac can come pick me up."

"I, um, I can just wait until everything clears up."

"It's not supposed to end until morning."

"Oh." Sammie looked out the window, turned her head and looked down at their clasped hands. Then she took a deep breath, letting the words fall from her lips before she lost her courage—or regained her senses.

"I could always just spend the night."

chapter TWENTY-SEVEN

Jonathan tossed the keys onto the small table by the door then stood there, his gaze on Sammie as she moved around the living room. She dragged her hand along the back of the recliner, fingered the edge of one of the throw pillows tossed on the sofa. Moving around the room, not bothering to take off her coat, not bothering to sit down.

Jonathan hesitated, thought about making a joke of inviting her to have a seat then thought better about it at the last minute. He couldn't judge her mood any better now than he could last night when he'd dropped Clare off. She was definitely preoccupied, but it was more than that. She seemed almost…shy. But it was more than that, too. It was like she was thinking, hard, and not coming to any conclusions.

At least, not any that she seemed happy about.

He moved through the living room and into the kitchen, pulling out coffee and filters then setting up the coffee maker. A few minutes later, the aroma of fresh-brewed coffee filled the kitchen. It would be a few minutes more before enough was brewed to drink, so he moved back to the living room and propped his shoulder against the wall.

Sammie had stopped pacing but she was still wearing her coat—and a frown of concentration.

"Coffee should be ready in a few minutes if you wanted to take off your coat. Have a seat."

She jumped, as if she hadn't heard him come in, then turned to face him. Her smile was just a little too forced, her shoulders just a little too tense as she shrugged out of her coat.

"I can still take you home, you know. It's no trouble."

"No." She shook her head and lowered herself to the sofa, perching on the edge of it. She draped her coat over her lap then stared at it, her fingers toying with the zipper as she slid it up and down.

His gut twisted at the expression on her face: confused, lonely. The only thing he wanted to do was rush to her side and pull her into his arms. Hold her. Kiss away the frown. Just kiss her, until she forgot about everything except them, the way they were together. The way they used to be.

The way he wished they could be again.

But he didn't move. Gut instinct told him the worst thing he could do was go near her right now.

So he stayed where he was and forced a smile to his face and tried to infuse his voice with a little bit of humor. "Are you sure? Because you don't exactly look like you want to be here."

The humor fell flat, even to his own ears. He doubted Sammie noticed though, not with the way she kept staring at her hands, the way she kept playing with the zipper of her jacket. Up and down, over and over, the sound almost hypnotic.

And then she stopped and looked straight at him, the look in her eyes both sad and determined. "Why did you come back, Jon?"

He should have expected the question. Hell, he *had* expected it, wondered why she hadn't asked him two months ago when he first showed up. But she hadn't asked and he had stopped expecting it, thinking she didn't want to know, figuring she wasn't ready for the answer.

Was she ready now?

He ran a hand through his hair then down along the back of his neck, blowing out a deep breath. He took a step forward, stopped, stepped forward again then hesitated before he finally dropped into the recliner.

Was that disappointment in Sammie's eyes? Had she been expecting him to sit next to her? No, he shouldn't read anything into that, not now. He couldn't afford to.

"Jon? Why did you come back? Was it for work?"

"No." He shook his head to reiterate the answer then stared down at his clasped hands. "No, it wasn't for work. Daryl wanted to set the office up in northern Virginia. I convinced him here would be better."

"Why?"

Jonathan raised his head, his gaze moving to hers. Holding it, refusing to let her look away with the sheer force of his will—

And a ton of prayer.

"Because I wanted to be near you and Clare."

"But why? It's been almost three years, Jon. How

did you know I would even agree to see you? That I would agree to let you see Clare?"

"I didn't."

"Then why? Why take that chance?"

"Christ, Sammie. Really?" He pushed out of the recliner, ran both hands over his head as he paced around the small table. He came to a stop, jammed his hands into his pockets, and stared down at his ex-wife. "Because I love you. I never stopped. I told you that."

"But for all you knew, I had remarried."

"I knew you didn't."

Surprise widened her eyes. "You checked on me?"

Should he feel guilty? Yeah, probably. But he didn't. And he told her as much. Was that a mistake? He didn't know, couldn't tell because she was looking down at the coat in her lap. Playing with that stupid fucking zipper again. What should he do now? Take her in his arms? Kiss her until she realized how much she still meant to him? Tell her that he wasn't going anywhere, that she could take all the time that she needed?

That he'd still be here, no matter what she decided?

What would he do if she decided she wanted nothing more to do with him? Fuck, it would kill him. Just *thinking* about that possibility made his gut clench and bile creep up the back of his throat.

But he wouldn't force her to decide, wouldn't play games with her to make her give him another chance. This—whatever she decided, whenever she decided—had to be up to her. It had to be *her* choice. He'd taken that away from her once, he'd be damned if he'd do it again.

Even if he had to wait the rest of his life for her.

He stepped back, needing to put a little more distance between them before he did something totally hypocritical, like pulling her off the sofa and kissing her senseless. Yeah, as tempting as that was—because fuck, he wanted nothing more than to kiss her again, touch her, hold her—he couldn't do that to her. He couldn't do that to either one of them.

"Come on, I'll take you home."

He expected her to nod. To stand up and shrug into her coat and walk to the door. Instead, she tossed her coat off her lap and stood up and walked toward *him*, not the door. One step. Two. Another and another until she was standing in front of him, so close he could feel the heat from her body brush against his. And it would be so easy to reach out, to brush that silky curl from her cheek and tuck it behind her ear, to lean down and kiss her. So fucking easy. But he didn't. He couldn't, not when he was afraid to move, damn near afraid to breathe.

It was Sammie who finally reached out, pressed the palm of her hand against his chest, right over his heart.

Her heart. It had always been hers. Had he ever told her that? Yes, years ago. A lifetime ago. Did she still know? Or had she forgotten?

"I hated you for so long, for what you did." Her voice was a ragged whisper, the words slicing through him. The breath hitched in his chest and his vision blurred. He blinked, trying to bring everything into focus, but it was no good. The only thing he could see was Sammie, staring up at him with tears in her eyes.

"Sammie—" He wanted to stop her, needed to tell her that he *knew*, that she didn't need to say the words. If he heard them, actually heard her tell him how much she hated him, it would kill him on the spot. But his throat wouldn't work and the words wouldn't come, no matter how much he struggled to say them.

"I thought I'd hate you forever. I wanted to. God, I wanted to. But..." Her voice trailed off. Hope flared to life in his chest, melting some of the icy fear that had been strangling him.

"But—?"

Sammie gazed up at him, tears filling those wide beautiful eyes, so deep he could lose his soul in them. He *had* lost his soul in them, years ago.

No, he corrected—he had found his soul.

"I'm scared, Jon. Scared that I don't hate you, when I know I should. Scared that I trust you, when I know I shouldn't."

"Sammie—"

Her hand drifted up his chest to his mouth. She placed two fingers over his lips, silencing him. "And I'm scared of what I feel. Terrified of how much I still love you."

"Sammie. God. I—" Jonathan cleared his throat, trying to clear the lump permanently lodged there. He finally moved, stepping closer, and reached out to cup her face between his hands. He stroked her cheek with his thumb, brushing away the single tear marring her perfect skin. "You're not the only one who's afraid. Loving someone that much—that gives them so much power over you. You've always held that power. Don't you know that?"

He reached for her hand and guided it to his chest, held it over the frantic beating of his heart. "Can't you feel it? My heart has always been yours, for as long as I can remember. God, Sammie. Without you, I'm nothing. I have no soul without you because you *are* my soul. You always have been."

"Then how could you have walked away like that? How could you have turned your back on us?"

"Because I was afraid. I thought you'd be better off without me. Thought you deserved so much more. I—I thought part of me had died over there, Sammie. After everything I did…I didn't want you to be stuck with someone half-dead."

"Jon, what you did over there, you did because you had to. You did to survive. To save lives. How could you possibly think that would change how I felt?"

"I—I don't know. I just—God, Sammie, things were so fucked up. And I couldn't bear the thought of coming home and having you look at me like I was some kind of monster, knowing what I did—"

"You're not a monster, Jon. You never were. And I just wish—" Sammie closed her eyes and took a deep breath, her chest rising and falling from the force of it. She opened her eyes and another tear fell, the sight of it tearing him apart. "I wish we could have that time back. That those years were never gone. But we can't get them back."

"No, we can't." Could she see what it cost him to admit that? See how much those lost years ate at him? He tightened his hand around hers and pressed it even closer, holding it tight against his heart. "But we can start over, can't we? Start over and make sure we live every minute for all we can."

"I—" Sammie hesitated, staring up at him while she chewed on her lower lip. He told himself to stay quiet, to not say a word. This was her decision to make. Her choice.

But his resolve to stay evaporated between one breath and the next. He couldn't stay quiet, not when there was so much riding on this. Sammie was too important to him, he couldn't risk staying quiet.

"I love you, Sammie. I never stopped. I wasn't lying about that. And I want you in my life. You and Clare both But if you can't—if you decide you don't want—" His voice cracked and he stopped talking for a second, cleared his throat and forced himself to keep going.

"If you decide this isn't what you want, I'm still going to love you. No matter what. And I'm always going to be here, waiting. Days. Weeks. Years. It doesn't matter. What I feel for you—it doesn't die. It never will."

Had he said too much? Had he scared her by telling her how he felt? Jonathan couldn't tell, not when she just stood there, staring up at him. He started to pull back, tried to tell her that he understood, that she could take all the time she needed.

Sammie stepped closer, leaning into him as she slid her hands around his neck. "I already know what I want, Jon. You. It's always been you. That's what scares me so much. And I don't want to wait. We've already wasted too much time. I don't want to waste anymore."

"Are you sure?"

Sammie nodded, the truth of her words—of her love—shining in her damp eyes. Jonathan leaned forward and captured her mouth with his. Soft, tender. Showing her with that one kiss how much she meant to him.

But it still wasn't enough. It would never be enough. He picked her up and carried her back to his bedroom, tried to show her with more than just kisses. More than just words.

And knew that a lifetime of loving her still

wouldn't be enough.

epilogue

The soft click of the door closing echoed in the quiet room, making Jonathan jump. He gave himself a mental shake, called himself a fool for being so nervous. Tried to tell himself there was no reason for him to be nervous.

Except there was—a million reasons, and the biggest one was standing in front of him, watching him with a small smile on her face.

Sammie stepped toward him and placed her hands against his chest. Sculpted brows arched over wide brown eyes that held a hint of laughter. His heart slammed against his breastbone as Sammie's fingers slowly worked the buttons of his dress shirt.

He closed his hands over hers, brought them to his mouth and brushed a gentle kiss along her knuckles.

Against the simple gold band on the ring finger of her left hand.

The wedding had been a small one, the informal ceremony held in an intimate ballroom of the hotel. Well, maybe not *small*, not with Sammie's entire team in attendance. But they didn't have any attendants—

just the bride and the groom and the flower girl, who kept giggling because she didn't understand why Mommy and Daddy were all dressed up, standing there in front of everyone.

Vows had been exchanged in low voices filled with emotion.

Filled with love.

Toasts had been made—more than one, as a matter of fact. Jonathan made a mental note to pay Mac and Daryl back for their toasts, even if they had caused the most charming blush he'd ever seen to stain Sammie's cheeks.

But the party was over now, at least as far as the bride and groom were concerned. Jonathan had swept Sammie into his arms and carried her out of the room, to the sound of cheers and applause.

There wouldn't be a honeymoon, not yet, not with Sammie's upcoming schedule. It was only January—they still had a few months left in their first season, not to mention the Blades' exhibition game against the Banners in two weeks.

That didn't mean Jonathan planned on skimping on the wedding night. Not even close.

He dipped his head and caught Sammie's mouth in a gentle kiss. Soft, sweet, with just a hint of promise of what was to come. Her hands slid up his chest, dipped inside the open edges of his shirt and traveled to his back. Touching. Caressing. Warm and gentle at first, then growing bolder. More insistent.

Jonathan eased his mouth from hers, pulled away just enough to rest his forehead against her own. "Do you have any idea how much I love you?"

Sammie's hand traveled from his back to his chest, not stopping until it rested over his heart. Her fingers trembled against his skin, touching something deep inside him, something so powerful, so potent, there were no words to describe it.

"As much as I love you."

The words echoed in Jonathan's mind, travelled to the deepest corner of his soul, and shattered the last bit of darkness there. Sammie loved him. He still couldn't believe it. After everything that happened, after everything he'd done…she loved him.

God knew he didn't deserve it. Sammie. Clare. This second chance. He didn't deserve any of it, didn't deserve *them*.

But he'd never let them go, never again. And he'd make damn sure that Sammie would never regret giving him this second chance. Every second, every minute, every day, for the rest of his life and beyond.

He caught her mouth with his again, this kiss anything but sweet. She leaned into him, sighed when he scooped her into his arms and carried her to the large bed.

And showered her with the beginning of a lifetime of love.

About the Author

Lisa B. Kamps is the author of the best-selling series *The Baltimore Banners*, featuring "…hard-hitting, heart-melting hockey players…" [USA Today], on and off the ice. Her *Firehouse Fourteen* series features hot and heroic firefighters who put more than their lives on the line and she's introduced a whole new team of hot hockey players who play hard and love even harder in her newest series, *The York Bombers*. *The Chesapeake Blades*--a romance series featuring women's hockey--launched in November 2017 with WINNING HARD.

Lisa currently lives in Maryland with her husband and two sons (who are mostly sorta-kinda out of the house), one very spoiled Border Collie, two cats with major attitude, several head of cattle, and entirely too many chickens to count. When she's not busy writing or chasing animals, she's cheering loudly for her favorite hockey team, the Washington Capitals--or going through withdrawal and waiting for October to roll back around!

Interested in reaching out to Lisa? She'd love to hear from you:

Website: www.LisaBKamps.com
Newsletter: http://www.lisabkamps.com/signup/
Email: LisaBKamps@gmail.com

Facebook:
https://www.facebook.com/authorLisaBKamps
Kamps Korner Facebook Group:
https://www.facebook.com/groups/1160217000707067/
BookBub:
https://www.bookbub.com/authors/lisa-b-kamps
Goodreads: https://www.goodreads.com/LBKamps
Instagram: https://www.instagram.com/lbkamps/
Twitter: https://twitter.com/LBKamps
Amazon Author Page:
http://www.amazon.com/author/lisabkamps

CROSSING THE LINE
The Baltimore Banners Book 1

Amber "AJ" Johnson is a freelance writer who has one chance of winning her dream-job as a full-time staffer: capture an interview with the very private goalie of Baltimore's hockey team, Alec Kolchak. But he's the one man who tries her patience, even as he brings to life a quiet passion she doesn't want to admit exists.

Alec has no desire to be interviewed--he never has, never will. But he finds himself a reluctant admirer of AJ's determination to get what she wants...and he certainly never counted on his attraction to her. In a fit of frustration, he accepts AJ's bet: if she can score just one goal on him in a practice shoot-out, he would not only agree to the interview, he would let her have full access to him for a month, 24/7.

It's a bet neither one of them wants to lose...and a bet neither one can afford to win. But when it comes time to take the shot, can either one of them cross the line?

Turn the page for an exciting peek at *CROSSING THE LINE*, available now.

"Oh my God, what have I done?" AJ muttered the phrase under her breath for the hundredth time. She wanted to rub her chest but she couldn't reach it under the thick pads now covering her. She wanted to go home and curl up in a dark corner and forget about the whole thing.

Me and my bright ideas.

"Are you going to be okay?"

AJ snapped her head up and looked at Ian. The poor guy had been given the job of helping her get dressed in the pads, and she almost felt sorry for him. Almost. Between her nervousness and the threat of an impending migraine, she was too preoccupied to muster much sympathy for anyone else right now.

"Yeah, I'm fine." She took a deep breath and stood, wobbling for only a second on the skates. This was not how she had imagined the bet going. When she cooked up the stupid idea, she had figured on having a few days to at least practice.

Well, not really. If she was honest with herself, she never even imagined that Alec would agree to it. But if he had, then she would have had a few days to practice.

So much for her imagination.

She took another deep breath then followed Ian from the locker room. It didn't take too long for her gait to even out and she muttered a thankful prayer. She only hoped that she didn't sprawl face-first as soon as she stepped on the ice.

Her right hand clenched around the stick, getting used to the feel of it, getting used to the fit of the bulky glove—which was too big to begin with. This would have been so much easier if all she had to do was put on a pair of skates. She had never considered the possibility of having to put all the gear on, right down to the helmet that was a heavy weight bearing down on her head.

She really needed to do something with her imagination and its lack of thinking things all the way through.

AJ took another deep breath when they finally reached the ice. She reached out to open the door but was stopped by Ian.

"Listen, AJ, I'm not even going to pretend I know what's going on or why you think you can do this, but I'll give you some advice. Shoot fast and low, and aim for the five and two holes—those are Alec's weak spots. The five hole is—"

"Between the legs, I know." AJ winced at the sharpness of her voice. Ian was only trying to help her. He had no reason to realize she knew anything about ice hockey, and not just because she liked to write about it. She offered him a smile to take the bite from her words then slammed the butt of the stick down against the door latch so it would swing open. Two steps later and she was standing on a solid sheet of thick ice.

AJ breathed deeply several times then slowly made her way to the other side of the rink, where Alec was nonchalantly leaning against the top post of the net talking to Nathan. They both watched as she skated up to them and came to a smooth stop. Alec's face was expressionless as he studied her, and she wondered what thoughts were going through his mind. Probably nothing she really wanted to know.

Nathan nodded at her, offering a small smile. She had to give the guy some credit for not laughing in her face when she asked his opinion on her idea. "Well, at least it looks like you've been on skates before. That's a plus."

AJ didn't say anything, just absently nodded in his direction. The carefree attitude she had been aiming for was destroyed by the helmet sliding down over her forehead. She pushed it back on her head then glanced at the five pucks lined neatly on the goal line. All she had to do was get one of them across. Just one.

She didn't have a chance.

She pushed the pessimistic thought to the back of her mind. "So, do I get a chance to warm up or take a practice shot?"

Alec sized her up then briskly shook his head. "No."

AJ swallowed and glanced at the pucks, then back at Alec. "Alrighty then. A man of few words. That's what I like about you, Kolchak." AJ though he might have cracked a smile behind his mask but she couldn't be sure. She sighed and leaned on her stick, trying to look casual and hoping it didn't slip out from under her and send her sprawling. "So, what are the rules?"

"Simple. You get five chances to shoot. If you score, you win. If you don't, I win." Alec swept the pucks to the side with the blade of his stick so Nathan could pick them up. She followed the moves with her eyes and tried to ignore the pounding in her chest.

She had so much riding on this. Something told her that Alec was dead serious about being left alone if she lost. It had been a stupid idea, and she wondered if she would have had better luck at trying to wear him down the old-fashioned way.

She studied his posture and decided probably not. He had been mostly patient with her up to this point, but even she knew he would have reached his limit soon.

"All or nothing, then. Fair enough. So, are you ready?"

AJ didn't hear his response but thought it was probably something sarcastic. She sighed then turned to follow Nathan to the center line, her heart beating too fast as her feet glided across the ice. She shrugged her shoulders, trying to readjust the bulk of the pads, and watched as Nathan lined the pucks up.

He finished then straightened and faced her, an unreadable expression on his face. He finally grinned and shook his head.

"I have no idea if you know what you're doing or not, but good luck. You're going to need it."

"Gee, thanks."

Nathan walked across the ice to the bench and leaned against the outer boards, joining a few of the other players gathered there. AJ wished they were gone, that they had something better to do than stand around and watch her make a fool of herself.

Well, she had brought it on herself.

She closed her eyes and inhaled deeply, pushing everything from her mind except what she was about to do. When she opened her eyes again, her gaze was on the first puck. Heavy, solid...nothing more than a slab of black rubber...

Okay, so she wasn't going to have any luck becoming one with the puck. Stupid idea. AJ had never understood that whole Zen thing anyway.

She swallowed and began skating in small circles, testing her ankles as she turned first one way then another, testing the stick as she swept it back and forth across the ice in front of her. Not too bad. Maybe she hadn't forgotten—

"Sometime today would be nice!"

AJ winced at the sarcasm in Alec's voice and wished she had some kind of comeback for him. Instead she mumbled to herself and got into position behind the first puck. She didn't even look up to see if he was ready. Didn't ask if it was okay to start, she just pushed off hard and skated, the stick out in front of her.

This was her one shot, she couldn't blow it.

PLAYING THE GAME
The York Bombers Book 1

Harland Day knows what it's like to be on rock bottom: he was there once before, years ago when his mother walked out and left him behind. But he learned how to play the game and survived, crawling his way up with the help of a friend-turned-lover. This time is different: he has nobody to blame but himself for his trip to the bottom. His mouth, his attitude, his crappy play that landed him back in the minors instead of playing pro hockey with the Baltimore Banners. And this time, he doesn't have anyone to help him out, not when his own selfishness killed the most important relationship he ever had.

Courtney Williams' life isn't glamorous or full of fame and fortune but she doesn't need those things to be happy. She of all people knows there are more important things in life. And, for the most part, she's been able to forget what could have been--until Harland gets reassigned to the York Bombers and shows back up in town, full of attitude designed to hide the man underneath. But the arrogant hockey player can't hide from her, the one person who knows him better than anyone else. They had been friends. They had been lovers. And then they had been torn apart by misunderstanding and betrayal.

But some ties are hard to break. Can they look past what had been and move forward to what could be? Or will the sins of the past haunt them even now, all these years later?

Turn the page for a preview of PLAYING THE GAME, the launch title of The York Bombers, now available.

The third drink was still in his hand, virtually untouched. He glanced down at it, briefly wondered if he should just put it down and walk away. It was still early, not even eleven yet. Maybe if he stuck it out for another hour; maybe if he finished this drink and let the whiskey loosen him up. Or maybe if he just paid attention to the girl draped along his side—

Maybe.

He swirled the glass in his hand and brought it to his mouth, taking a long sip of mostly melted ice. The girl next to him—what the fuck was her name?— pushed her body even closer, the swell of her barely-covered breast warm against the bare flesh of his arm.

"So you're a hockey player, right? One of Zach's teammates?"

Her breath held a hint of red wine, too sweet. Harland tried not to grimace, pushed the memories at bay as his stomach lurched. He tightened his grip on the glass—if he was too busy holding something, he couldn't put his arm around her or push her away— and glanced down. The girl looked like she was barely old enough to be in this place. A sliver of fright shot through him. They did card here, right? He wasn't about to be busted picking up someone underage, was he?

She had a killer body, slim and lean with just enough muscle tone in her arms and legs to reassure him that she didn't starve herself and probably worked out. Long tanned legs that went on for miles and dainty feet shoved into shoes that had to have heels at least five inches tall. He grimaced and briefly wondered how the hell she was even standing in them.

Of course, she *was* leaning against him, her full breasts pushing against his arm and chest. Maybe that was because she couldn't stand in those ridiculous heels. Heels like that weren't meant for walking—they were fuck-me heels, meant for the bedroom.

He looked closer, at her platinum-streaked hair carefully crafted in a fuck-me style and held in place by what had to be a full can of hairspray—or whatever the fuck women used nowadays. Thick mascara coated her lashes, or maybe they weren't even her real lashes, now that he was actually looking. No, he doubted they were real. That was a shame because from what he could see, she had pretty eyes, kind of a smoky gray set off by the shimmery eyeshadow coloring her lids. Hell, maybe those eyes weren't even real, maybe they were just colored contacts.

Fuck. Wasn't anything real anymore? Wasn't anyone who they really claimed to be? And why the fuck was he even worried about it when all he had to do was nod and smile and take her by the hand and lead her out? Something told him he wouldn't even have to bother with taking her home—or in his case, to a motel. No, he was pretty sure all he had to do was show her the backseat of his Expedition and that would be it.

Her full lips turned down into a pout and Harland realized she was waiting for him to answer. Yeah, she had asked him a question. What the hell had she asked?

Oh, yeah—

"Uh, yeah. Yeah, I play hockey." He took another sip of the watery drink and glanced around the crowded club. Several of his teammates were scattered around the bar, their faces alternately lit and shadowed by the colored lights pulsing in time to the music.

Jason pulled his tongue from some girl's throat long enough to motion to the mousy barmaid for a fresh drink. His gaze caught Harland's and a wide grin split his face when he nodded.

Harland got the message loud and clear. How could he miss it, when the nod was toward the girl hanging all over him? Jason was congratulating him on hooking up, encouraging him to take the next step.

Harland took another sip and looked away. Tension ran through him, as solid and real as the hand running along his chest. He looked down again, watched as slender fingers worked their way into his shirt. Nails scraped across the bare flesh of his chest, teasing him.

Annoying him.

He put the drink on the bar and reached for her hand, his fingers closing around her wrist to stop her. The girl looked up, a frown on her face. But she didn't move her hand away. No, she kept trying to reach for him instead.

"What'd you say your name was?"

"Does it matter?" Her lips tilted up into a seductive smile, full of heated promise as her fingers wiggled against his chest.

Did it matter? It shouldn't, not when all Harland had to do was smile back and release her hand and let her continue. Or take her hand and lead her outside. So why the fuck was he hesitating? Why didn't he do just that? That was why he came here, wasn't it? To let go. Loosen up. Hook up, get things out of his system.

No. That may be why Jason and Zach and the others were here and why they brought him along—but that wasn't why he was here. So yeah, her name mattered. Maybe not to him, not in that sense. He just wanted to know she was interested in *him* and not what he did. That he wasn't just a trophy for her, a conquest to be bragged about to her friends in the morning.

He gently tightened his hand around her wrist and pulled her arm away, out of reach of his chest. "Yeah. It matters."

Something flashed in her eyes—surprise? Impatience? Hell if he knew. He watched her struggle with a frown, almost like she didn't want him to see it. Then she pasted another bright smile on her face, this one a little too forced, and pulled her arm from his grasp.

"It's Shayla." She stepped even closer, running her hand along his chest and down, her finger tracing the waistband of his jeans.

He almost didn't stop her. Temptation seized him, fisting his gut, searing his blood. It would be easy, so easy.

Too easy.

Then a memory of warm brown eyes, wide with innocence, came to mind. Clear, sharp and almost painful. Harland closed his eyes, his breath hitching in his chest as the picture in his mind grew, encompassing soft brown hair and perfect lips, curled in a trembling smile.

"Fuck." His eyes shot open. He grabbed the girl's hand—Shayla's—just as she started to stroke him through the worn denim. Her own eyes narrowed and she made no attempt to hide her frown this time.

"What are you doing?" Her voice was sharp, biting.

"I could ask you the same thing."

Her hand twisted in his grip. Once, twice. "Zach told me you needed to loosen up. That you were looking for a little fun."

Zach had put her up to this? Harland should have

known. He narrowed his eyes, not surprised when the girl suddenly stiffened. Could she see his distaste? Sense his condemnation? He leaned forward, his mouth close to her ear, his voice flat and cold.

"Maybe you want me to whip my cock out right here so you can get on your knees and suck me off? Have everyone watch? Will that do it for you?"

She ripped her hand from his grasp and pushed him away, anger coloring her face. "You're a fucking asshole."

Harland straightened and fixed her with a flat smile. "You're right. I am."

She said something else, the words too low for him to hear, then spun around and walked away. Her steps were short, angry, and he had to bite back a smile when she teetered to the side and almost fell.

Loathing filled him, leaving him cold and empty. Not loathing of the girl—no, the loathing was all directed at himself. What the fuck was his problem?

The girl was right: he was a fucking asshole. A loathsome bastard.

Harland yanked the wallet from his back pocket and pulled out several bills, enough to cover whatever he'd had to drink and then some. He tossed down the watered whiskey, barely feeling the slight burn as it worked its way down his throat. Then he turned and stormed toward the door, ignoring the sound of his name being called.

He should have gone home, back to the three-bedroom condo he was now forced to share with the sorry excuse that passed for his father. But he wasn't in the mood to deal with his father's bullshit, not in the mood to deal with anything. So he drove, with no destination in mind, needing distance.

Distance from the spectacle he had just made of himself.

Distance from what he had become.

Distance from who he was turning into.

But how in the hell was he supposed to distance himself…from himself?

Harland turned into a residential neighborhood, driving blindly, his mind on autopilot. He finally stopped, eased the SUV against the curb, and cut the engine.

Silence greeted him. Heavy, almost accusing. He rested his head against the steering wheel and squeezed his eyes shut. He didn't need to look around to know where he was, didn't need to view the quiet street filled with small houses that showed years of wear. Years of life and happiness and grief and torment.

"Fuck." The word came out in a strangled whisper and he straightened in the seat, running one hand down his face. Why did he keep coming here? Why did he keep tormenting himself?

She didn't want to see him, would probably shove him off the small porch if he ever dared to knock on the door. He knew that, as sure as he knew his own name.

As sure as he knew that she'd be sickened by what he had become. Three years had gone by. Three years where he'd never bothered to even contact her. Hell, maybe he was being generous. Maybe he was giving himself more importance than he deserved. Maybe she didn't even remember him.

He rubbed one hand across his eyes and took in a ragged breath, then turned his head to the side. The house was dark, just like almost every other house on the block. But he didn't need light to see it, not when it was so clear in his mind.

A simple cottage style home, with plain white siding that was always one season away from needing a new coat of paint. Flowerbeds filled with exploding color that hid the age of the house. A small backyard filled with more flowers and a picnic table next to the old grill, where something was always being fixed during the warmer months.

An image of each room filled his mind, one after the other, like a choppy movie playing on an old screen. Middle class, blue collar—but full of laughter and warm memories. He knew the house, better than his own.

He should. He'd spent more time here growing up than he had at his own run-down house the next street over. He had come here to escape, stayed because it was an oasis in his own personal desert of despair.

Until he had ruined even that.

He closed his eyes against the memories, shutting them out with a small whimper of pain. Then he started the truck and pulled away, trying to put distance between himself and the past.

A past that was suddenly more real than the present.

Made in the USA
Middletown, DE
30 August 2019